"I'm very glad you're home safe and sound."

Blake's shoulders lifted and fell in a dismissive gesture.

"You believe me, don't you?" she urged.

He surveyed her anxious face with a measure of surprise. "Don't sound so serious, Juliana. Of course I believe you. Is there any reason I shouldn't?"

"Well, I...well, you...I mean...I wouldn't like you to think I would ever want you dead."

"Of course I don't think that!" He chuckled, though a little darkly. "You could get everything you want by simply divorcing me."

MIRANDA LEE is Australian, living near Sydney. Born and raised in the Bush, she was boarding-school educated and briefly pursued a career in classical music before moving into the world of computers. Happily married, with three daughters, she began writing when family commitments kept her at home. She likes to create stories that are believable, modern, fast-paced and sexy. Her interests include reading meaty sagas, doing word puzzles, gambling and going to the movies.

Books by Miranda Lee

Don't miss any of our special offers. Write to us at the following address for information on our newest releases.

Harlequin Reader Service
U.S.: 3010 Walden Ave., P.O. Box 1325, Buffalo, NY 14269
Canadian: P.O. Box 609, Fort Erie, Ont. L2A 5X3

MIRANDA LEE

Marriage in Jeopardy

Harlequin Books

TORONTO • NEW YORK • LONDON
AMSTERDAM • PARIS • SYDNEY • HAMBURG
STOCKHOLM • ATHENS • TOKYO • MILAN
MADRID • WARSAW • BUDAPEST • AUCKLAND

ISBN 0-373-11728-0

MARRIAGE IN JEOPARDY

Copyright © 1993 by Miranda Lee.

First North American Publication 1995.

CHAPTER ONE

THE first inkling Juliana had that something was wrong came with Stewart's telephone call to her office. Not that this was unusual. Blake's secretary often called her to relay messages from her husband. It was Stewart's tone of voice that disturbed her. He sounded almost . . . rattled.

'Mrs Preston, have you by any chance heard from Mr Preston today?' he asked after announcing himself.

'No, Stewart, I haven't. Why? Is there some problem?'

His hesitation to answer sent Juliana snapping forward on her chair. 'What is it?' she said sharply. 'What's happened?'

Her anxious quizzing seemed to shock Stewart back into his more characteristic role as Blake's unflappable right-hand man. 'No need to be alarmed, Mrs Preston,' he replied in that maddeningly phlegmatic voice he usually used. It's just that when I rang the Sydney office a minute ago they hadn't seen hide nor hair of Mr Preston all day. The manager sounded most relieved, I might add.'

'The *Sydney* office? Why would Blake be in the Sydney office? Wasn't he flying straight home from Manila today?'

'You mean Mr Preston didn't tell you of his change of plan?'

Juliana bit her bottom lip in a vain attempt to stop dismay from swamping her. This was one aspect of her marriage that had been bothering her more and more of late. Blake's obsession with personal space. He hated answering to anyone, especially his wife. Juliana knew *why* this was so, but knowing why did not make it any easier to bear.

'No, Stewart,' she admitted. 'He didn't.'

'I see.' The secretary was unable to hide the sardonic edge in his voice.

What do you see? Juliana agonised with a rush of fierce emotion. A marriage without love? A woman prepared to accept any kind of treatment in exchange for money and position?

Her heart ached with the desire to explain that her relationship with Blake was not really like that. OK, so maybe their marriage *had* been entered into with their heads, rather than their hearts. But that didn't mean they didn't care for each other, that they hadn't become the most important people in each other's lives.

If she came across as a cool, reserved spouse then that was because Blake liked her that way. Surely Stewart could appreciate that. He himself had been hired as Blake's secretary and assistant because he possessed the very qualities Blake demanded in all those close to him. He was self-sufficient, self-reliant, self-contained. Like herself.

Only she didn't feel self-contained at that moment. She felt extremely vulnerable. And worried.

'Please, Stewart,' she went on, her voice unsteady. 'Don't leave me in the dark. Tell me what's going on.'

Once again, the man hesitated. Clearly, he'd been well trained by Blake over what the boss's wife should and shouldn't know.

Juliana felt the beginnings of panic. '*Please*,' she pleaded. Oh, God, if something had happened to Blake she didn't know what she would do.

'Mr Preston will be very cross with me,' the man muttered, 'but I suppose you have a right to know since my call has obviously upset you. Your husband sent me a fax yesterday to say he'd finished in Manila a day early and had decided to drop off at our Sydney branch for a totally unannounced visit on the way home, but that he would still be arriving in Melbourne by five-thirty.'

'But you said he *hasn't* dropped in at the Sydney office!'

'Which is no reason to panic, Mrs Preston. As you well know, it's not unlike your husband not to let even me know of last-minute changes of plans. Maybe he's stayed on in Manila. Or maybe he's gone to the Brisbane office instead. He's sure to turn up at Tullamarine airport as per schedule. The boss is very reliable like that. I'll just mosey on out to the airport to meet him and you pop on home and dress for dinner. I've booked a table for you and Mr Preston at Don Giovanni's for eight-thirty.'

'But what if his plane doesn't arrive?' Juliana cried, unable to think of something as ridiculous as dressing for dinner when for all she knew her Blake might be in mortal danger.

'It will, Mrs Preston. Be assured of that. Now do stop worrying, and please ... let this incident be our little secret. Your husband would be far from pleased if he knew I'd bothered you with this minor misunderstanding. Do I have your reassurance that you won't mention it to him?'

Juliana sighed. 'I suppose so, but please call me at home as soon as Blake's plane touches down, otherwise I'll worry myself to death.'

'I'll certainly do that, Mrs Preston,' he finished with far more warmth than usual.

Juliana hung up, aware that nothing would make her feel better till Blake was home again, safe and sound. Three weeks he'd been away. Three long, lonely weeks. She'd been so looking forward to tonight, to dinner, then afterwards. Now ...

Her heart squeezed tight. What if something awful had happened? What if she never saw Blake again?

I'm being maudlin, she told herself abruptly. Maudlin and melodramatic and ridiculous. Just because I've been having some small doubts about my marriage lately. Stewart's right, Blake does this sort of thing all the time. He'll show up as he always does, smoothly elegant and totally unruffled. There's absolutely no reason to worry, let alone panic.

Still, Juliana could not settle to any more work that afternoon and was glad to leave the office at four-thirty, anxious to be home for Stewart's call. The Preston mansion was only a few miles from the city, overlooking the Eastern side of Port Phillip

Bay, but Juliana caught the Friday afternoon rush, and the drive home took over an hour.

The telephone was ringing as she let herself into the house via the garages shortly after five-thirty. Since it was Mrs Dawson's night off, there was no one to answer it, and Juliana hoped it would keep ringing till she could reach the closest extension. Hurrying through the laundry and into the kitchen, she dropped her coat and handbag on the breakfast counter and snatched the receiver down from the wall. 'Yes?'

'Mrs Preston?'

'Stewart! Oh, thank God you didn't hang up. I was just letting myself in and I ran. But everything's all right now,' she sighed happily. 'Blake's jet landed on time, I gather?'

'Well—er——'

Juliana froze.

'Mr Preston's plane *hasn't* arrived as yet, I'm sorry to say, and I've been having some trouble locating him. I've been in contact with Manila, and it seems Mr Preston left on time yesterday, with Sydney as his intended destination, but the airports there are insistent he did not land anywhere in Sydney at all either yesterday or today.'

All the blood began draining from Juliana's face. 'Dear heaven...' She dragged over a kitchen stool and slumped down on it before she fell down. 'Have...have you contacted the various authorities?'

'I certainly have. They're making enquiries.'

'Making enquiries,' she repeated limply.

'Please try not to worry, Mrs Preston. I'm sure everything will be all right.'

'Do...do you think I should come out to the airport myself?'

'I don't think that would be wise,' came the firm advice. 'Especially if Mr Preston arrives shortly, as I'm sure he will. You know how he hates being fussed over. He'd much prefer you to wait for him at home, as you always do.'

Juliana flinched at what sounded like a reproof. The only reason she didn't meet or see her husband off at airports was because he always insisted she didn't, not because she didn't want to. This was another aspect of her marriage that was beginning to trouble her: other people's perceptions of it. Still, this was hardly the time to be worrying about appearances.

'You promise to ring me,' she said shakily, 'as soon as you know anything? Anything at all.'

'I promise, Mrs Preston. Must go. Bye.'

Juliana finally hung up the receiver. Oh, God...Blake...

For a moment she buried her face in her hands, terrified by the images that kept bombarding her mind. Blake...lying dead in a twisted mangle of metal on some mountainside. Blake...sinking to the bottom of the ocean in a cold coffin of steel. Or worst of all...his beautiful body charred beyond all recognition. Planes often burst into flames when they crashed.

Her loud cry of utter desolation shocked even herself.

Juliana's lovely hazel eyes opened wide. She sat up straight in the stool. Dear heaven, she thought with a wild churning of her stomach. Dear heaven . . .

Juliana sat in the dark in her living-room, all alone. She was grateful that it was Mrs Dawson's night off, grateful that she didn't have to put up with the woman's scepticism over her distress. Blake's housekeeper had made it perfectly plain without being overtly rude that she didn't approve of her employer's wife, always calling Juliana 'Mrs Preston' in a stiffly formal manner.

Two hours had passed since Stewart's call. It felt like two years.

The sudden sound of the phone ringing sent Juliana leaping to her feet. Heart pounding madly, she raced across the room, hesitating fearfully before snatching the dreaded instrument up to her ear. 'Yes?'

'Stewart Margin here again, Mrs Preston. No need to worry any longer. Mr Preston is perfectly all right.'

Juliana swayed, gripping the edge of the telephone table as a steadier. 'Oh, thank the lord,' she whispered huskily. 'Thank the lord . . .'

She closed her eyes for a second to say another private prayer of thanks. Blake hadn't been killed in a plane crash after all! Soon he would breeze in through their front door, splendid as always in one of his immaculate business suits. He would toss aside his crocodile-skin briefcase before reefing his tie off then heading straight for the drinks cabinet where he would pour himself a hefty Scotch and call out to her. 'Come and join me, Juliana, and tell me about your day. Mine's been hell!'

Oh, Blake... What would I have done if something had happened to you? How would I have survived?

She paled as the realisation that had come to her earlier on struck again with sickening force, a realisation which could threaten her future happiness almost as much as Blake's dying. A small sob escaped her throat, her knuckles whitening as her nails dug into the wood.

'Mrs Preston? Are you all right?'

No, she cried in silent anguish. I'm not all right. I'm never going to be all right again. Don't you see? Somewhere along the line I've fallen in love with my husband! Why, if he walked in right now I would throw myself into his arms, weeping and making a complete fool of myself.

And what would Blake do? He would stare down at me in appalled horror, coldly withdrawing from such a display of emotional possessiveness. Oh, how he hated women who clung, who needed, who *loved* like that.

God! Whatever am I going to do?

Ask about your husband, you little idiot, the voice of common sense suggested. But ask *calmly*.

She gulped and set about gathering her wits. For if she didn't she might as well ask Blake for a divorce this very night.

'I am now,' she assured Blake's secretary. 'Has my husband's plane actually arrived?'

'No. He's coming in on a commercial flight that lands in ... let's see now ... in about ten minutes' time.'

'A *commercial* flight? What happened to his Learjet? Did it break down somewhere?'

'In a way. It appears that some time after take-off from Manila yesterday Mr Preston's plane went through a cloud of volcanic dust that clogged up the engines—and the on-board electronics—so badly that the pilot had to make an emergency landing.'

'An emergency landing? But *where*? Why weren't we *told*?'

'Fortunately the pilot knew of an American air-force strip on a nearby island, but unfortunately it was abandoned. It took some time for them to be able to contact authorities and get a helicopter to take them back to Manila. Blake had a message sent through to Tullamarine airport but it was misplaced temporarily during a change-over of staff. It's always rather hectic here during Friday evening peak hour. Not that that's any excuse really. Still, all's well that ends well, Mrs Preston. The boss is safe and sound.'

For the second time that day Juliana heard traces of emotion in Stewart Margin's voice. So he too had been worried. And he too was relieved.

A softly ironic smile passed over her lips. And why wouldn't he be? Without Blake as company director, Preston's Toys and Games would probably quickly revert to the almost bankrupt business it had been when he'd taken over a few years before.

Without Blake, Stewart Margin might be swiftly without a job.

Without Blake...

Juliana shivered. If only her own relief weren't tinged with this awful apprehension.

If only this incident hadn't happened at all! she agonised. Then she might never have realised the depth of her feelings. She would have been able to go on in blissful ignorance, happily being the sort of wife Blake wanted without worrying that any moment she might betray herself and, in doing so, lose him.

But have you been happy being that sort of wife? came a dark voice from deep inside. *Really* happy? What about all those niggling little doubts of late?

'Mrs Preston? Are you sure you're all right?'

Juliana scooped in a steadying breath. 'I *am* still a little shaken,' she admitted. 'I'll be fine by the time Blake arrives home. But, as you mentioned earlier, my husband does hate any fuss, so best he doesn't know the extent of my concern over this matter.'

'Of course, Mrs Preston. I wouldn't *dream* of telling him.'

'Good. Let me know if there are any more delays, will you?'

'Certainly.'

When Juliana hung up the phone she didn't know whether to laugh or cry. She felt both elated and devastated. In the space of a couple of hours she had been through an emotional mill. She was *still* going through it.

She turned to walk somewhat dazedly out into the deserted kitchen, switching on the electric kettle for a cup of coffee. Would Blake still want to go out for dinner when he got home? she wondered distractedly.

She doubted it. He was sure to have been fed on the plane.

There was one thing, however, that he might want tonight after being away for so long.

Juliana shuddered. An odd reaction, she realised, for a woman who had found nothing but pleasure in her husband's arms.

But with her newly discovered love burning in her heart Juliana could see that the intimate side of their marriage left a lot to be desired. Blake conducted their sex-life in a coolly clinical fashion, without any spontaneity or real passion. They had separate bedrooms, their sexual encounters always pre-arranged. He even marked the calendar in his study with the dates on which she would be...indisposed. Being on the Pill, Juliana could provide this information in advance.

She wished now that this were one of those days. But it wasn't.

Of course she could *understand* Blake's aversion to sharing a room with her. It was his way of keeping her at a safe distance, making sure she didn't start demanding any more than he was prepared to give.

But *understanding* did not make the situation sit better around her heart.

She cringed now to think of the way Blake would give her the nod before retiring whenever he wished to sleep with her; the way he didn't come into her room till she was showered and already in bed; the way he never stayed the whole night with her, going back to his own room once he was finished.

Juliana shook her head in distress. God, it was little better than legal prostitution.

No, no, she denied quickly. That was being unfair to Blake and their marriage. Their sex-life was only one aspect of their relationship. They were partners in more ways than just in bed. They went everywhere together. They were good friends. They always had been.

Was she going to ruin what they had simply because she'd been silly enough to fall in love? She would be crazy to. Her marriage was stronger than most. They were going to try for a baby next year. Madness to throw that all away by wanting the one thing she couldn't have.

So Blake didn't love her. He *did* care for her in his own peculiar way. So he wasn't swept away by passion for her at odd times during the day. He *did* make love to her quite beautifully when he came to her bed. And that was often enough.

For pity's sake, what did she want out of life? She had it good, had what she'd always wanted. Financial security; a solid marriage; a good job. All she had to do was keep her love under control and simply go on as before.

Which included not making any objections to the way Blake conducted their sex-life.

But, dear heaven, she hoped he would be too tired to come to her bed tonight. She didn't think she could bear to have him touch her just now. She was sure to do something silly, sure to give herself away.

There again, she did so long to hold him. Just hold him.

But Blake didn't know how to just be held. He never, ever touched Juliana at all except when he climbed into her bed. Not for him the simple holding of hands or the putting of an affectionate arm around her shoulder or waist. He was not, and never would be, a toucher.

And Juliana knew why.

Bitterness rose in her chest. His mother had a lot to answer for.

The telephone ringing again cut through the silence of the house.

Juliana stiffened.

It was Blake. She just *knew* it was Blake, ringing before he left the airport.

Though never liking her to call him at all, he often phoned her. It was another of his quirks about wives which Juliana fully understood. His mother had driven his father crazy with constant telephone calls, especially when he was away on business. They had not been chatty, affectionate calls, but jealously possessive calls, always wanting to know where he was, what he was doing, where he was going, when he would be home.

Then, once he *was* home, she never let him out of her sight, always touching him, kissing him, pawing at him. Noreen Preston had been a neurotically insecure women who'd loved her handsome husband to her—and everyone else's—distraction.

Juliana knew all this, not because Blake had told her. Her mother had told her. Her mother, who had been the live-in cook here in the Preston household for almost twenty years, her long employ coming to an abrupt halt a year ago when she was accidentally killed by a hit-and-run driver.

Juliana closed her eyes against the rush of tears. Poor Mum...

Yet she knew her mother would not have wanted her pity. Or her grief. Lily Mason had been an open-hearted, kind-natured woman who'd embraced life with a naïve optimism that left little room for regrets and remorse. Unfortunately, however, this same naïve optimism made her vulnerable to certain types of men, ones whom Lily always thought loved and needed her.

All they had loved and needed, Juliana thought bitterly, was her mother's quite beautiful body in bed. Not one of them had ever offered to support her, or marry her, not even Juliana's father, who had apparently disappeared into the wide blue yonder as soon as he'd found out his teenage girlfriend was pregnant.

At least Lily hadn't made the mistake of letting any of these men live with herself and her daughter. Juliana was spared that. But even as a young child tucked up in bed she'd heard her mother sneaking men into her room late at night.

This had stopped for a while when Lily and her daughter had moved into the flat above the Prestons' garage. But not for long. Lily merely moved her assignation time to during the day,

Juliana often smelling male aftershave and cigar smoke when she came home from school.

The insistent ring of the telephone brought Juliana back to reality. What on earth was she doing, mentally rumaging over all this dirty linen? The past might hold explanations for why people did what they did—herself and Blake included—but it didn't give her any weapons with which to handle the present and the future.

All she could do was gather herself and answer the telephone, and, if it was Blake, show him that nothing had changed between them. Nothing at all.

She reached up and lifted the receiver down to her ear, telling herself to act as if she were taking a business call at work. As public relations officer for a large international cosmetic company Juliana had had plenty of practice at appearing cool under stress.

'Juliana Preston,' she said with superb calm.

'Blake here, Juliana.'

'Blake!' she exclaimed with a forced lilt in her voice. 'You bad man, you had me so worried.' Her tone betrayed not the slightest hint of any real worry.

He laughed his attractively lazy laugh, reinforcing her belief that this was the way to play the situation.

'And there I'd been,' she went on lightly, 'thinking you'd made me into a premature widow.'

'Thinking, or hoping?' he drawled. 'And don't you mean a *merry* widow? I'm worth a bundle. Even more after the deals I've just made.'

Juliana's skin crawled at the mention of money. It was bad enough having people like Stewart and Mrs Dawson believing she'd married Blake for his money, worse to have her husband voicing the same opinion.

Maybe it had been partly true. Once. But not now. Not any more...

How ironic that Blake would hate to think that was so. He *liked* the arrangement they had come to, the sort of marriage he'd insisted upon and which Juliana had thought she'd wanted too, at the time. God! If only she were able to take him into her confidence, to tell him of her newly discovered love.

But that was impossible. He didn't want her to love him. In fact, he would hate the idea. The truth was, if she wished to continue being Mrs Blake Preston she would have to hide her love behind the sort of wife she'd successfully been up till now, but which she suspected would prove hard to be in the future.

'Everything went well, then?' she asked, keeping her voice amazingly cool.

'Fantastic!' he returned. 'I love doing business with the Asians—they're a real challenge.'

She forced a laugh. 'And how you do like a challenge!'

'Do I?'

'You know you do. That's the only reason you came back into the fold of the family business. Because it was on the skids. You liked to think you could resurrect it from the ashes like the phoenix.'

He chuckled. 'You could be right. But aren't you going to ask me what happened to my plane?'

'Stewart gave me the general idea. You can tell me more later.'

'Such restraint. Sometimes, Juliana,' he said with a dry laugh, 'I almost think you don't love me.'

Her heart squeezed tight. 'Whatever would give you that idea?' she tossed off.

He laughed again. 'Can I hope you'll be a bit more enthusiastic about my return later tonight?'

All her insides tightened. 'I would have thought you'd be too tired for that after your little adventure.'

'I slept on the plane.'

The implication behind his words was clear. He wasn't too tired. He would definitely be coming to her bed tonight.

Oddly enough, this thought didn't produce the reaction in Juliana that she might have expected, given her earlier apprehension. It actually sent a hot wave of desire racing through her body, bringing a flushed heat to her face.

She was shocked. She wasn't the easiest woman to arouse, Blake always having to take his time before she was ready for him. She suspected that her mother's promiscuous behaviour had instilled in her an instinctive fear of appearing sexually easy—hence the difficulty she had always found in surrendering her body to a man. Even with Blake, who seemed to know exactly what to do to relax, then excite her, she was still somewhat inhibited. There were several sexual activities and positions she not only would not permit, but which had previously repelled her.

Now, Juliana could hardly believe the images that kept flashing into her mind, or the way her heart was racing.

Had falling in love within the security of marriage finally released in her the sort of sensuality Lily's daughter should always have possessed? Had she subconsciously locked a highly sexed nature away within a tightly controlled shell, for fear of turning out like her mother?

Perhaps. Only time would tell, she realised shakily. Time. And tonight...

'Maybe I'll have a headache,' she said, seeking to defuse her tension with humour.

'I'll bring some aspirin home with me,' Blake countered drily.

'What if I just said no?'

'You never have before.'

'Maybe I've found somebody else to keep me happy while you're away.'

Blake laughed. 'Is that so? Well, you'll just have to tell him your hubby's home and he isn't needed any more. Now I suggest you have a nice relaxing bath and I'll be with you as soon as I can.'

After his abrupt hanging-up, Juliana stared down into the dead receiver, not sure how to take Blake's amused indifference to her taunt about another man. It crossed her mind that he might react the same way even if she hadn't been joking.

Wouldn't he *care* if she had an affair? she worried with a sudden and quite dampening dismay. Was he himself doing the same with other women during his business trips away?

She had never thought to question his faithfulness before, had never been ripped to pieces inside by the shards of jealousy that were even now slicing deeply into her heart. The thought of him touching another woman as he touched her...

A violent shudder ran through her before she was able to pull herself together with some solid reasonings.

Blake had *never* given her a reason to be jealous on his business trips. It wasn't as though he ever took a female secretary or assistant with him. He didn't have one. His faithful Girl Friday was a man—Stewart.

OK, so he didn't ring her every single day as some husbands would. And he never brought her a gift home, to show that he had been thinking of her while he was away.

But she fully understood why he didn't do either of those things.

Once he arrived home he always showed her in bed how much he had missed her, never missing a night for at least a week. Would he be like that if he was having other women on the side? No, of course not, Juliana reasoned. His offhand response was just his being as flippant with her as she had been with him. She was imagining things.

But her imaginings demonstrated perhaps what was to be feared in falling in love. She could almost understand Blake's deep aversion to it. Love made you irrational, panicky, insecure. Especially when that love was not returned.

The automatic kettle made a click as it switched itself off. Juliana stared at it. She didn't feel like coffee any more. A swift glance at the wall-clock showed it was ten to nine. Blake could be here in a little over an hour.

She shivered again. What to do?

Perhaps she should have that bath he'd told her to have. It might relax her, calm her nerves.

Juliana moved slowly from the living-room out into the large foyer from which the semi-circular staircase rose in all its magnificent glory. Hesitating for a moment on the first step, her hand curled over the knob at the end of the elegantly carved balustrade, Juliana's mind slipped back nineteen years to the first time she actually saw this house, and this imposing staircase.

Who would have dreamt that the little girl who had stared with open-mouthed awe at the riches contained within the hallowed walls of the Preston mansion would one day be mistress of that same house? And who would have believed that she would ever find herself in the same situation as the tragic Noreen Preston, in love with a husband who didn't love her back?

For a moment, Juliana's stomach churned. But then she straightened her spine and continued up the stairs.

There was one major difference between herself and Noreen Preston. *She* was from tougher stock. Far tougher. No way would she ever commit suicide because she found out her husband was having an affair with another woman. She would fight for what she wanted, fight to the death.

And, as of now, she wanted Blake. More than she could ever have envisaged.

CHAPTER TWO

HALF an hour later, Juliana was lying in her bath, remembering that there had once been a time when she and Blake had been so close, she could have told him anything. But of course that had been years ago, and so much had changed since then . . .

The first time Juliana saw Blake he'd frightened the life out of her. She'd only been nine at the time. It was on her mother's second day as cook in the Preston household. Mr and Mrs Preston had kindly given Juliana permission to use their swimming-pool and, since it was an awfully hot day, smack-dab in the middle of the summer holidays, she had been only too happy to accept their generous offer.

So, garbed in her cheap multi-coloured costume, Juliana made her way out on to the vast back patio and pool complex. And it was while she was gaping at the Olympic-size pool, complete with extravagant surroundings, that the accident happened.

Blake, then fifteen, was making his first attempt at a backward somersault from the diving-board. Apparently, he didn't jump far enough away from the end of the board, for he banged the back of his head during the turn, splashing into the water then sinking like a stone to the bottom.

'Blake!' screamed a girl who was lying sun-bathing on a deckchair. Juliana was to find out later that she was Blake's eleven-year-old sister, Barbara.

But for now Juliana's attention was all on the unconscious shape at the bottom of the pool.

She didn't stop to think. She simply dived in, dog-paddled down to him and dragged him up to the surface. 'H...help me!' she spluttered out to Barbara, who was standing open-mouthed by the side of the pool.

Somehow, with her inept help, Juliana managed to pull Blake out.

'He's dead!' his sister cried. 'Oh, my God, he's dead.'

'No, he's not,' Juliana refuted, though frightened that he might be. 'Go and tell my mum to ring an ambulance!' she ordered. 'The *cook*!' she screamed when Barbara looked blankly at her. 'My mum's the new cook!'

Barbara ran while Juliana set about doing what she'd seen on television a few times but which she had no real experience with: mouth-to-mouth resuscitation. But she must have done something right, for by the time her mother ran out to tell her the ambulance was on its way Blake started coughing back to consciousness. By the time the paramedics arrived he only needed a little oxygen to be on the way to full recovery.

'I reckon you saved his life, little lady,' one of the paramedics praised.

'Really?' she grinned, widely pleased with herself.

'Yes, really,' the man said. 'Your mum should be very proud of you.'

Behind the ambulance officer's back Barbara pulled a face at Juliana, which set the tone of their relationship from that day forward. Barbara never let an opportunity go by to express her disgust and disapproval that the cook's child was allowed the run of the house, let alone *her* pool. Blake, however, immediately became Juliana's firm ally, defending her against Barbara's bitchy snobbery and generally being very nice to her.

Oddly enough, despite the six-year age-difference, he really seemed to find Juliana's company enjoyable. Maybe because she was a bit of a tomboy, and would join in with his leisure activities. They swam together, dived together, played board games together. Juliana also believed he found her a pleasant change from all Barbara's girlfriends who went ga-ga over him all the time. He clearly found their drippy drooling both embarrassing and repugnant.

Still, Juliana wasn't blind. She could see that at fifteen Blake was a well-grown and very handsome young man. His blue-eyed blond looks and well-shaped bronzed body drew the girls in droves. Barbara's classmates found any excuse to visit the Preston household. Not that he ever took any notice of them. They were too young for him, for a start. Generally speaking, he didn't seem to like girls at all. If he *did* have any girlfriends during his high-school years, he kept them a secret.

Juliana was the only female given the privilege of Blake's company and conversation, much to Barbara's friends' pique. They repaid her in a myriad spiteful little ways, from openly insulting her background to pretending to be friendly before cutting her dead. Once they even gave her an invitation to a non-existent birthday party.

Juliana could still remember her humiliation when she turned up at the address, only to be bluntly told there was no party there that day. Not wanting to upset her mother—who'd been so pleased by the invitation—she spent all afternoon in the park before returning home and pretending the party had been fantastic.

It was only when she told Blake later about the incident and he gave her a look of such pained apology that she finally burst into tears. He hugged her, something he *never* did, and told her not to worry, that people like that would eventually get their come-uppance.

But Juliana privately believed the privileged rich rarely got their come-uppance. It was the working-class poor who always suffered, who were put upon and discriminated against. The rich never lived in back rooms or wore hand-me-down clothes. They certainly didn't know what it was like not to be able to go on school excursions because they didn't have the money.

By the time Juliana turned twelve she'd decided that one day she was going to be rich too.

'When I grow up,' she told Blake shortly after her twelfth birthday, 'I'm going to marry a millionaire.'

Blake glanced up from his desk with a surprised look on his face. 'I don't believe you said that. I thought you despised the wealthy.'

Juliana was lying face-down on his bed, her face propped up in her hands. 'I'm going to start a different brand of wealthy. I'll give a lot of my money to charity and be kind to my servants.'

'What do you mean, be kind to your servants?' he said sharply. 'Mum and Dad are kind to your mother. Besides, you always said people shouldn't *have* servants at all.'

'Employees, then,' she argued stubbornly. 'I'll have to employ someone to clean and cook for me. I'm going to have a career.'

'Why have a career,' he scoffed, 'if you're going to marry for money? Rich men's wives don't work. They have lunches and their hair done.'

'I'm going to be different.'

'Are you, by gum?' He laughed at last.

'Yes, I am!'

'And what if you can't find a rich man to marry you?' he mocked. 'The rich marry the rich, or didn't you know that?'

Juliana frowned. She hadn't thought of that. But she wasn't about to have her dream shattered by cold, hard reality. Sitting up abruptly, she tossed her long straight brown hair back over her skinny shoulders, her pointy chin lifting defiantly. 'I'm going to be so beautiful when I grow up that millionaires will be hammering at my door!'

'*You*! *Beautiful*?'

His laughter cut to the quick. For Juliana knew she was a bit of a scarecrow, with her long, bony body and equally long, bony face. Only her eyes carried any promise of future beauty, being slanty and exotic-looking, their colour a chameleon hazel which changed colour with whatever she was wearing.

'You wait and see,' she pouted. 'My mother says I'm going to grow up quite lovely. She says I could be a model with my height and bone-structure.'

'Your mother has rose-coloured glasses,' Blake muttered. 'About everyone and everything.'

'You leave my mother alone. She's a fantastic person. You're just jealous because your mother hasn't time for anyone except your father!'

'I don't give a damn about my mother,' he scowled. 'Now get lost, rake-bones. I've got to get on with this study.'

'You're always studying these days,' she complained.

'Yeah, well, I want to grow up smart, not beautiful. My HSC is in a couple of months and I have to get well over four hundred to get into my course at uni next year. So for pity's sake get out of here, Juliana, and let me get some work done.'

She flounced out, thinking grouchily to herself that he didn't have to grow up beautiful because he already was, the lucky devil!

Juliana's dream of even becoming passably attractive came to an abrupt halt the following year. Puberty came in a rush and, horror of horrors, she broke out in a bad case of acne. All of a sudden she felt so ugly and awful that during her spare time she remained hidden in her bedroom. To make matters worse, that same year her mother sent her to the same toffee-nosed private school Barbara went to, the result of having saved like a lunatic during her four years' employ at the Prestons'.

Little did Lily know that the sacrifices she had made for her much loved child's future were not bringing Juliana much present happiness. She was going through hell during her first year of high school among the daughters of millionaires. Never before had the difference between her world and the world of wealth and privilege been so painful. The children of the rich did not tolerate outsiders kindly.

The acne was the last straw for Juliana. Oh, how she would cry when she looked at herself in the mirror every morning. She was absolutely hideous!

Her only reprieve was that Blake was away on campus at university, doing his first year of an economics and law degree. She was afraid he might tease her about her skin. It was bad enough having Barbara calling her names like 'pizza-face' on the way to and from school every day.

But Blake was to be home soon on his mid-term break, and Juliana was simply dreading the day he would come over and call up to her to come swimming with him.

The day dawned, however, and when she refused to come down from the flat above the garages Blake thumped up the stairs, banged on the door and demanded to know what was the damn matter with her.

'I'm not leaving, Juliana,' he pronounced forcefully. 'So you might as well come out here and tell me what's what. And don't give me any garbage about your not liking the water any more because I won't believe you.'

Wretched with embarrassment and misery, she finally opened the door.

'Well?' he said, looking her in the face with only puzzlement on his.

'Can't you *see*?' she wailed.

'See what?'

'My skin,' she groaned.

The light dawned in his eyes. 'Oh, you mean the acne.'

She looked down at the floor in an agony of wretchedness and frustration. 'Of course I mean the acne,' she grumbled.

He put out a hand and tipped up her chin, scanning her face. 'They're not that bad, sweetie,' he said so tenderly that she promptly burst into tears.

'They are too!' she sobbed, and struck away his hand. 'What would you know? You've never had a pimple in your life! They're ugly. I'm ugly.'

Blake sighed. 'You're not ugly, Juliana. Fact is, I suspect you're going to become the beauty you always wanted to be. Why, you've grown so tall and graceful this past year. And you're not nearly as skinny as you used to be,' he added, flicking a rueful glance at her sprouting breasts. 'But if you're so unhappy with your skin, why don't you do something about it?'

'Like what? Mum says there's not much I can do except keep it clean. She said I'll grow out of it in God's own good time.'

'God helps those who help themselves,' he said sharply. 'Come on. I'm taking you to the doctor. I know there are things they can do for acne these days.'

'Do you really think so?' Juliana said hopefully.

'I know so!'

An hour later she came home armed with an antibiotic lotion for her skin which the doctor said had proved very successful with other patients, particularly girls. Juliana set about using it morning and night, and it wasn't long before she saw a quite dramatic improvement.

'It's a miracle!' she exclaimed to Blake in the pool a week later.

'I don't believe in miracles,' he returned with such a dark scowl that Juliana was taken aback. She frowned at him. He'd changed since going to university, she realised with a pang of true regret. Why did people have to change? First herself, and now Blake.

Her eyes followed him as he swam over to the edge of the pool and levered himself out of the water, the action showing a muscle structure in his back and arms she'd never noticed before.

'Have you been doing weights?' she asked.

He shrugged. 'A little. They have a good gym at the uni. It keeps me out of trouble.'

'What kind of trouble?'

His blue eyes flashed with exasperation, but he said nothing.

Juliana swam over and scrambled out to sit next to Blake, blushing when she noticed that one of her nipples had popped out of the tiny bra-top. She stuffed it back in, relieved that Blake wasn't looking at her.

There was no doubt about it, though. She would have to ask her mother for a new costume before the swimming carnival at school next week. This one was getting too small for her rapidly growing body.

'Can I feel your muscles?' she asked Blake, dripping water all over his thighs as she bent over to curve her hands around his biceps. 'Gosh, they're really something. Your back looks fantastic too.'

When she ran a quite innocent hand across his shoulder-blades, Blake stiffened. 'Cut it out,' he snapped, then abruptly dived into the pool.

Juliana stared after him, hurt and confused. What had she done?

But then she sighed her understanding. She'd touched him. Blake hated girls touching him.

Still, she would have thought he didn't think of her as a girl, just as she never thought of him as a boy. They were simply good friends.

It wasn't long, however, before Blake put aside his aversion to girls touching him. A never-ending stream of nubile young women began accompanying him whenever he came home from university.

Blondes, brunettes, redheads—Blake didn't seem to have any preference. The only thing the girls had in common was that none of them lasted very long. A few weeks at most.

At first Juliana had felt a sharp jealousy, for Blake never seemed to have time for her any more. But gradually her feelings changed to bitter resignation. Her close relationship with the son and heir to the Preston fortune had drawn to a close. She was once again nothing more than the cook's daughter, whose presence was tolerated though no longer sought out.

Only once during her school years did she cross Blake's path in anything other than a 'hi, there, how's things, see you later' fashion. It was to prove a very memorable experience.

She was sixteen at the time. It was the night of her graduation ball to which she had worn Barbara's gown of two years before, given to her mother by an uncharacteristically sweet-tongued Barbara.

'Mummy paid a fortune for this, Lily,' she said as she handed over the exquisite ivory satin gown. 'It seems a shame that it's only been worn once. I'm sure Juliana would look divine in it. Much better than I did. She's so tall and slender.'

Naturally, her kind-hearted and still amazingly naïve mother had not seen the malice behind the offer. All she could see was a dress that she would never be able to afford for her own daughter, a dress fit for a princess.

'Just think, Juliana,' she had said excitedly. 'You'll be able to use the money I was going to spend on your dress to have your hair done and to buy a really good pair of shoes. Maybe an evening bag as well. Oh, you're going to look so beautiful!'

Lily would never have understood the fact that, at the fancy school she took such pride sending her daughter to, no girl would be seen *dead* in a dress another graduate had worn before, no matter how beautiful it was. Though not of this snobbish ilk, Juliana nevertheless shrank from the thought of turning up in Barbara's dress, for Barbara would make sure every girl in her class, as well as their partners, knew whose dress it really was. Blake's sister had already gone to great pains to make sure

Juliana was treated like a leper by most of the other girls at school.

But Juliana wouldn't have hurt her mother for the world. So she staunchly wore the dress, ignored the other girls' snide remarks, holding her head high and looking as though she didn't give a damn what anyone said about her. Her cool, even haughty demeanour gave the impression that their snide remarks and sniggering whispers rolled off her like water off a duck's back.

Behind the cool façade, however, lay a deep well of hurt and anger. What right did they have to treat her like this, just because she hadn't been born into money? It wasn't fair! One day, she vowed, she would spit in their eyes, *all* of them—especially Barbara!

She left the ball as early as she could, but she couldn't go home. Her mother would be waiting up for her, anxious to hear the details of the night. So Juliana slipped quietly round the back of the main house instead of going straight up to bed, intent on filling in an hour or two just licking her wounds in private. Barbara and Mrs Preston were away for the night at relatives'. Mr Preston would be ensconced in his study at the front of the house. The pool area would be deserted.

So she was startled to find Blake sprawled in one of the deckchairs, for he wasn't expected home for the summer holidays till the following day.

Juliana quickly noted the whisky glass in his hand and the half-empty bottle of Jack Daniels on the cement beside the chair. This was another of his new habits. Drinking. Though it was usually only beer.

'Well, well, well,' he drawled, his eyes raking over her. 'Is this Cinderella home from the ball? And what a lovely Cinderella she is,' he went on in his now habitually droll fashion. University—or maybe life—had turned Blake into something of a cynic.

For once, Juliana found a retort just as cynical. 'I have no doubt the role of Cinderella fits me very well. But I can't see your sister as my Fairy Godmother, can you?'

Blake's eyebrows shot up in surprise at her acid tone. 'Meaning?'

'Barbara kindly presented my mother with her old graduation dress for me to wear tonight.'

'Aah ... I see ...'

'Do you, Blake? Have you any idea what it's like being treated like a charity case? No, of course not! You were born with a silver spoon in your mouth.'

'Sometimes one can choke on a silver spoon,' he said darkly, and quaffed back a huge mouthful of drink.

'I haven't noticed *you* choking. Not unless it's on grog,' she added, sweeping over to stand at the foot of the deckchair with her hands on her hips. 'What on earth are you doing, swallowing that whisky like water? Haven't you any respect for your kidneys and liver?'

He swung his legs over the side of the chair and stood up, tall and macho in tight, stone-washed jeans and a chest-hugging blue T-shirt. 'I'm not large on respect tonight,' he muttered.

'And what is *that* supposed to mean?'

'Nothing I can tell you, gorgeous.'

She drew in a sharp breath as his blue eyes moved hotly down her body to where the deep sweetheart neckline of the dress showed an expanse of creamy cleavage. Not a busty girl, Juliana's breasts were nevertheless high-set and nicely shaped. Blake's gaze was certainly admiring them at that moment. His narrowed gaze eventually moved on, travelling down to where the ivory silk ballgown hugged her tiny waist before flaring out into a romantically full, ankle-length skirt.

'That dress looks a damn sight better on you than Barbara,' he said thickly.

His gaze lifted to her face, shocking her with the stark desire she saw in their depths. No boy—or man—had ever looked at her like that before. Blake certainly hadn't.

'Juliana,' he said hoarsely, before doing something that both shocked and fascinated her. Dipping his finger into the glass he was still holding, he reached out to trace a wet trail around the neckline of her dress. This alone made her stand stock-still with eyes wide and heart suddenly pounding. But when he bent his head to start licking the liquid from her by now shivering flesh, a dizzying sensation made her sway backwards. He caught her to him, releasing the glass for it to smash into smithereens on to the concrete around their feet.

His head bent to kiss her with such deceptive gentleness that Juliana was momentarily disarmed. He sipped at her lips, over and over, his hands lifting to slide up into her hair, to lift its heaviness from her skull, his fingertips massaging her head with an almost hypnotically erotic action.

'Juliana,' he whispered against the melting softness of her lips.

'Yes?' came her dazed query.

'Yes,' he repeated huskily. 'That's all you need to say. Yes. I think you could be very good at yes...'

His mouth turned hungry, his lips prising hers apart. But when his tongue slid inside, the strong taste of whisky blasted her back to reality.

She wrenched her mouth away and glared up at Blake, furious with both herself and him.

His eyes were glazed as they opened to look down at her. 'What is it, honey? What's wrong?'

'You're drunk, Blake Preston! That's what's wrong.'

His eyes cleared to an expression of dry amusement. 'So if I weren't drunk, it would be all right? You'd let me kiss you?'

'Yes...no... Oh, don't be silly, Blake. You know we can never be anything but friends. Rich men don't become involved with the daughter of their cook! At least, not seriously!'

A black cloud darkened his face. He looked angry about something for a moment, then wearily resigned. 'I guess you're right.' A sardonic smile pulled at his mouth. 'So what's happened to your plan to marry a millionaire?'

'I know now that the only way I'll ever be rich is to earn it myself.'

'Oh? And how, pray tell? Your school marks have hardly been encouraging.'

'I'm going to study like a lunatic from now on. I can do it. I know I can!'

He cocked his head slightly on one side, staring at her for a few moments before giving a wry nod. 'Yes. I do believe you can. Come on, I'll walk you home...'

Juliana lay awake for ages that night, no longer thinking about the terrible time she'd had at the ball, or the white lies she'd told her mother when Blake delivered her to the door. Her mind was filled with memories of Blake's mouth moving over her cleavage, his strong arms pulling her hard against him, his tongue plunging between her lips.

Had it been the realisation of his drunkness that had made her stop him, or panic at the bewildering responses his actions had evoked in her body? She'd never felt anything like it before. There had been a rush of heat and excitement, combined with a momentary compulsive urge to let go every vestige of thought, to just let Blake do as he willed with her.

What bothered her most was that she seemed to have been responding to *Blake's* need, not her own. Why, she'd never looked upon him as anything more than a good friend before. She'd certainly never had any sexual fantasies over him as she had had over a few television and pop stars she liked. Yet all he'd had to do was look at her with desire in his eyes and she'd instinctively responded to that desire.

Juliana was stricken by the thought that maybe she was beginning to turn out like her mother, whose sexual vulnerability to men who *needed* her was quite pathetic in Juliana's opinion. She didn't want to be like that. She wanted always to be in control of her own actions, her own life. When and if she made love, she wanted it to be because *she* wanted and needed it, not the other way around. Anything else went against the grain!

By the time Juliana felt sleep snatching at her mind, she'd vowed to be on her guard against any repeats of tonight's incident. She would make sure she was never alone with Blake. She would keep other boys at arm's length as well, till she was older, and more in control of her silly self! She also vowed to do what she had boasted to Blake she would do— get a good pass in the Higher School Certificate, go to university and become a success, all by her own efforts!

Over the next two years she astounded both her mother and her teachers with her application. The boys did start hanging around, and even though she did find several of them quite attractive Juliana spurned their attentions, devoting all her time to study, and a smattering of modelling. Though she had not grown up into a classical beauty, her long, silky brown hair, tall, elegant body and exotically sculptured face gave her admission into a good modelling agency who found occasional work for her on the catwalk and behind the fashion photographer's lens.

After an excellent pass in her Higher School Certificate, Juliana began a marketing course at university, while still earning money from modelling on the side. Though not enough to live away from home. Blake, however, was doing well enough as a foreign exchange dealer to move out into a luxurious bayside unit. From gossip she had gleaned he'd quickly become quite the young man-about-town, working hard and playing hard.

It was while Juliana was doing her last year at university that tragedy struck the Preston household. Noreen Preston committed suicide with an overdose of sleeping tablets. Shortly afterwards, her husband Matthew succumbed to a heart attack, leaving behind a plethora of debts and a badly managed, almost bankrupt business.

Suddenly Blake and Barbara were parentless, and without any sizeable inheritance. Even the house carried a second mortgage. Barbara responded by marrying a middle-aged but very wealthy widower. Blake shocked everyone by chucking in his job, selling his flat and returning home to take up the flagging reins of the family company. With new ideas and a lot of hard work he eventually turned Preston's Games and Toys from an old-fashioned, non-profitable organisation into a modern, go-ahead concern whose stock was to become highly sought-after by investors and brokers all over the world.

By the age of thirty Blake Preston had become the toast of Melbourne's business and social worlds. Two years in a row he was voted Victoria's most eligible bachelor by a high-profile women's magazine.

He seemed to crown his worldly successes when he became engaged to Miss Virginia Blakenthorp, one of the débutante darlings of Melbourne's old-money families. It was around this time that Juliana herself—now gainfully employed in the marketing division of a chain of retail stores and living in a small but neat flat near the city—became engaged. To the younger son of the owner of the stores.

His name was Owen Hawthorne. He was twenty-eight and everything any woman could possibly want. Handsome. Polished. Rich.

It would have seemed that both Blake's and Juliana's futures were assured.

Yet one fateful night, the day before Juliana's twenty-sixth birthday and only a few weeks after her mother died, two engagements were broken and a third one entered into. Blake and Juliana were married a month later.

CHAPTER THREE

JULIANA was lying back in the bath, thinking about that strange night, when she heard Blake call out.

'Juliana! Where are you?'

She sat bolt upright, the abrupt action sending bubbles and water spilling over the edge on to the floor.

'I . . . I'm in here,' came her shaky reply. 'In the bathroom.'

Good God! she thought. Stewart must have driven like a lunatic to have dropped Blake off this early. Or had she been mulling over the past for longer than she realised? Since her wristwatch was out in the bedroom she had no idea of the exact time.

Juliana had just stood up to climb out of the bath when Blake opened the door and walked in.

'Julianna, I wish you'd . . .' His voice died when she swung round, giving him a full-frontal view of her nude body.

Wide-open hazel eyes found his startled blue ones. Juliana had never ever appeared naked like this before him. Not standing up. And certainly not with bubbles dripping from suddenly hard nipples. A fierce blush zoomed into her cheeks, her embarrassment finding voice in sharp words.

'For goodness' sake, Blake, haven't you ever heard of knocking?' In her haste to get out of the bath to wrap a towel around herself Juliana forgot about the water on the floor. As she hurriedly put one foot down on to the slippery tiles, it shot out from under her.

'Watch it!' Blake cried, racing forward to grab her. When she felt his hands close around her soap-slicked flesh she panicked, and tried to ward him off.

'Don't! I'm all right!'

But he already had a firm hold around her waist, lifting her right out of the water and setting her safely down on the mat in front of the vanity unit.

Did Blake deliberately slide his hands down over her bare buttocks before letting her go?

Juliana knew he probably didn't. Even so, her immediate sexual awareness produced further panic and every muscle in her body snapped tight as a drum.

'A towel,' she choked out. 'Get me a towel.'

Practically snatching the thing from his out-stretched hand, she wrapped it quickly around herself sarong-style. Only then did she appreciate that Blake was staring at her in puzzlement.

Juliana knew she was acting exactly the opposite of how she'd vowed to act.

Her covering smile was not as sweetly soothing as she would have liked. 'Thank you. I—er—hope I haven't ruined your lovely suit. It's all damp down the front.'

Blake glanced down at the pale grey three-piecer which he wore most often when travelling, brushing at the waistcoat lightly. 'It'd take more than a few drops of water to ruin this little number.'

Which was true. Worth a small fortune, the mohair- and silk-blend suit fitted his broad-shouldered, slim-hipped body like a glove and never creased, even after the longest flight. Matched as it was at the moment with a crisp white shirt and a darker grey tie, in it Blake looked both coolly suave and utterly in command of himself.

Not so Juliana. She felt a mess, both inside and out. All she could hope for was that Blake would get out of here shortly and give her some breathing space. Meanwhile...

'You must have had a good run from the airport,' she said brightly, 'to get here so quickly.'

'We did. Caught every green light.'

'I thought for a moment I might have lost track of the time.'

When Blake made no attempt to leave the room, simply moving over to lean casually against the white-tiled wall, Juliana turned to face the vanity unit, though still made uncomfortably aware of his presence by his reflection in the mirror. Since they didn't share a bathroom, each having their own, Juliana was not used to being watched going about her everyday ablutions. To have Blake do so at this particular moment in time was unnerving in the extreme.

'Wouldn't you like to go and have a drink while I clean my teeth and stuff?' she asked with another pained smile.

'No. I'd rather stay here and talk to you.'

'Oh... oh, all right.' She shrugged nonchalantly, fully aware that this was to be her first real test.

What would the Juliana of a few hours ago have done in the circumstances?

She had no idea. This particular circumstance had not even been in *that* Juliana's repertoire.

So what would a woman desperate to hide her love for her husband do?

Pretend he's not in the room at all, she told herself. Pretend you're quite alone. Pretend you're talking to him on an intercom.

Taking another of the fluffy cream towels from the nearby railing, she proceeded to dry her arms, then turned to lift one foot up on to the side of the bath. 'So tell me all about your little adventure,' she invited casually while she towelled down first one long, shapely leg then the other.

'Nothing much to tell, really. It—er—— Where on earth did you get those bruises?' he interrupted, straightening to frown down at three black and blue smudges on her thigh.

Juliana stared down at them as well, not having noticed them herself till now. 'I have no idea,' she said truthfully. 'Probably knocked into the side of a desk at work. You know how easily I bruise.'

'No,' he returned slowly. 'I don't, actually.'

Juliana was taken aback by the dark suspicion in his voice. Her surprise expressed itself in an edgy laugh. 'What on earth are you implying?'

She stared up at him, seeing a Blake she had never seen before. His face had an awful stillness about it, his normally lazy blue eyes narrowed and darkened till they were slits of cold steel.

Just as suddenly, however, his distrustful expression cleared, a sardonic smile dispelling the tightness around his mouth. He was his old self once more: coolly relaxed and casually indifferent.

'For a moment there I had a picture of you having a rather different encounter with a desk,' he drawled. 'I should have known better. You're not into that type of sex, are you?'

Juliana's face flamed.

Blake's pat on her cheek was both indulgent and quite patronising. 'My sweet, innocent Juliana. Who would ever have believed it? But I rather like you as you are. It's most ... reassuring. Still ...'

For a long moment, he just stared into her startled eyes, his hand lingering on her jawline. Juliana could have sworn that he was going to kiss her, the prospect filling her with both dread and the most appalling excitement.

Yes, kiss me, her pounding heart urged him. Kiss me, touch me, take me ...

Suddenly, his hand dropped away, his shoulders squaring. 'I think I *will* go down for a drink after all,' he said curtly. 'Join me when you're ready, if you like. If not ... I'll join you later.' And, turning abruptly, he strode from the room, leaving Juliana to lean weakly against the vanity unit. When she glanced up into the mirror it was to see wide, glittering eyes, and lips already apart.

She groaned, leaning forward on to curled fists, shutting her eyes against the evidence of her own arousal. God! Whatever was she going to do?

Fifteen minutes later, she was going downstairs, dressed in her favourite dressing-gown, a rather ancient dusky pink velour robe that crossed over the bodice and sashed around the waist. It had deep pockets that one could slide one's hands into and feel very cosy.

Juliana's hands were indeed slid into the pockets as she moved across the entrance hall and towards the main living-room, but she felt far from cosy. Petrified would be closer to the mark. Still, she *looked* relaxed. And that was the primary requisite at the moment.

When she moved through the archway and on to the plush grey carpet that covered the expansive living-room floor, Blake glanced up from where he was stretched out on one of the chesterfields, giving her a small smile of approval.

'It always amazes me how good you look without having to try. There you are, with your face scrubbed clean and your hair pinned haphazardly on top of your head, garbed in a robe that's seen better days, and you still look fantastic. Of course you do move very well,' he remarked, watching her walk into the room.

'And you do flatter very well,' was her cool rejoinder.

'I have no reason to flatter you, Juliana. You're my wife.'

'Oh, charming.'

His chuckle was as droll as her tone. 'So!' Placing his own generous drink on the glass coffee-table in front of him, Blake stood up. 'What will you have to drink?'

'Something strong,' she answered, not without a touch of self-mockery.

'That's not like you.'

A nonchalant shrug disguised her inner tension. 'It's been one hell of a day.'

Blake laughed. 'That's usually *my* line.'

Moving over to the antique rosewood sideboard they used as a drinks cabinet, he picked up the decanter of whisky and filled a clean crystal tumbler to halfway. Then came several ice-cubes from the silver bucket, cracking as Blake plopped them into the drink.

'This should soothe any frayed nerves you have.' He walked over to where Juliana was standing with her back to the empty fireplace. 'Here...'

She had to take both of her hands out of the shelter of the robe's pockets to accept the glass safely, cupping it firmly so that the drink wouldn't rattle. 'Thank you.'

'That's OK. Come and sit down.'

'I'd rather stand.'

Again, he darted her a sharp look. 'You *are* feeling out of sorts, aren't you? Anything I can help you with?' he asked as he retrieved his drink and joined her by the fireplace.

'Not really. Things didn't go as smoothly as I would have liked with a new product launch this week, that's all,' she exaggerated.

'What went wrong?'

'Oh, nothing major,' she hedged. 'Certainly nothing as dramatic as what happened to you yesterday. Want to fill me in on the details? You weren't in any real danger, were you?'

His lop-sided smile was rueful. 'Let's just say there were a few moments when I thought I might have to change my underwear.'

Juliana's stomach contracted. For Blake to admit as much meant he'd been very close to death and disaster. Very close, indeed.

'I . . . I'm glad you're home safe and sound.'

Blake's shoulders lifted and fell in a dismissive gesture.

'You *believe* me, don't you?' she urged with a weird flash of fear.

He surveyed her anxious face with a measure of surprise. 'Don't sound so serious, Juliana. Of course I believe you. Is there any reason I shouldn't?'

'Well, I...well, you...I mean...I wouldn't like you to think I would ever want you dead.'

'Of course I don't think that!' He chuckled, though a little darkly. 'You could get everything you want by simply divorcing me.'

She stared as he lifted his glass and quaffed a huge swallow. If she'd wanted evidence of Blake's current attitude to their marriage, she'd just got it. Nothing had changed since the night he'd proposed. Not a thing!

Her sigh was heavy as she lifted her own glass to her lips and drank.

'Tired?' he asked.

'A little.'

'Not *too* tired, I hope.'

'No...' There was a decided lack of conviction in that word.

A sudden strained silence pervaded the room, the only noise the clink of Blake's ice as he drained his glass.

'I think I'll go upstairs and have a shower, then,' he announced, depositing his empty glass on the mantelpiece behind them and striding from the room.

Several seconds later Juliana realised she was holding her breath. She also realised that, no matter how iron-clad her resolve to carry on as though nothing had changed in their relationship, there was one aspect where that was not possible. When Blake came to her bed tonight, it wasn't going to be the same. Not at all.

Would it be agony or ecstasy?

Either outcome worried the life out of her. For while Blake's lovemaking had always pleasured her, she'd never wanted it with this intensity before; had never been *afraid* of what her responses might be. She'd always been content to let Blake make the running, to just be swept along on *his* tide, never her own. Now, she'd discovered that love had its own tide.

Already, waves of desire were racing through her veins, their current strong and relentless. Never again would Juliana want to lie submissive beneath Blake, waiting resignedly for him to rouse her senses to an almost reluctant passion. She suspected that in future she would have to struggle to control a wildly escalating need for all sorts of intimacies, to hold herself in check lest she actually devour the man.

Common sense told her this was the last thing she should do.

Expelling the air from her lungs in a ragged rush, Juliana looked for fortification—and intoxication—in the glass her quivering hands were holding. A few swift swallows and it was empty, save some small bits of unmelted ice.

Whisky had always hit her system hard and fast, making her mellow. And yes... sometimes quite sleepy. Juliana hoped tonight would be no exception.

No such luck. The whisky, if anything, seemed to spark a recklessness in her.

Why shouldn't I devour Blake if I want to? came the rebellious thought as she swept up the stairs. He's my husband, after all. Why should I hold back, pretend, fake being *less* passionate than I feel like being? It's crazy! Blake would probably be thrilled if I became more adventurous and aggressive in bed. A man of his experience and sophistication couldn't possibly be totally satisfied with our rather bland sex-life.

But no sooner had she decided this than another more sensible and quite insistent voice whispered to Juliana that Blake *was* satisfied; that he would look upon any change in her sexual behaviour with definite disapproval.

Juliana hesitated at her open bedroom door, her gaze ignoring the rest of the exquisitely furnished room to focus on the brass bed that sat proudly against the far wall. Queen-sized and fit for a queen, with its superb antique cream lace bedspread and hand-painted ceramic postknobs, Juliana's bed had once been Noreen Preston's bed.

Thank the lord she hadn't died in it, came the unexpected thought. Noreen's body had been found in a seedy motel on the other side of Melbourne.

Still, Juliana suspected that a lot of wretchedness had been fostered between those sheets. If she closed her eyes she could almost hear the poor woman crying; *see* her clinging.

Odd. Juliana had never felt any real sympathy for Noreen Preston before, the woman having always come across as a neurotic wife and simply dreadful mother. But one never knew the hidden secrets in a marriage, the whys and wherefores behind people's behaviour.

Had the handsome and selfish Matthew Preston enjoyed putting his wife through mental hell? Had he taken advantage of her obsessive love for him by greedily accepting all her attentions while callously dallying behind her back? Had he laughed at her insecurities, telling outrageous lies? Or had he thrown his infidelities in her face, till she couldn't bear any more?

'Juliana...'

She swung round at Blake's voice behind her, a nervous hand fluttering up to her throat. 'You startled me.'

'I didn't mean to.'

Her eyes flicked down over him, trying not to stare.

Some men might have looked funny in the fluffy white towelling robe Blake always wore after showering. He didn't, however. He looked gorgeous, the white colour emphasising the warm golden tan of his satin-smooth skin. If he'd been dark and hairy, the knee-length, open-necked style might not have been quite so flattering. But the adult Blake was no more dark and hairy than the adolescent Blake had been. He still looked like a young golden god, Juliana thought wryly. Her own private Adonis.

'What's the matter, Juliana?'

Blake's unexpected question snapped her eyes up to his. Had she been staring too much? Frowning, perhaps? Grimacing, even?

Juliana recognised that her heart was pounding madly in her chest. There was no doubt about it. She *would* devour him. The realisation forced her to a decision.

'Actually, Blake, I'm not feeling the best. I really *do* have a headache.'

His steady gaze was disturbingly unreadable.

'It's been getting worse all day,' she went on in quiet desperation. 'First with the problems at work, and then after Stewart called I...I...' She swallowed. 'I was very worried about you, Blake. For a while there I was beginning to think the worst.'

'Is that so? As you can see, though...' he spread his arms wide for a second '...I'm fine.'

'And I'm very happy and relieved you are, but the after-effect of worry is often a headache. Look, you did ask me what was wrong, and I'm telling you.'

'So you are,' he said in a curiously flat voice. 'I'll see you in the morning, then.'

'*Morning*?' she repeated, eyes blinking wide. Blake had never come to her bed in the morning.

His smile was dry. 'For breakfast, Juliana. We usually breakfast together on a Saturday morning, remember?'

Her face flushed with an embarrassed heat. 'Yes, of course. I...I forgot. Tomorrow's Saturday...'

'Don't forget to take some pain-killers before you go to bed,' he advised curtly.

'I won't.' His message was quite clear. Don't have a headache tomorrow night...

Taking her by the shoulders, he planted a cold kiss on her forehead. 'Goodnight, Juliana. Sleep well.'

Again she heard the hidden message. You sleep well, wife, because I certainly won't. I wanted some sex tonight and you turned me away.

Juliana felt rotten. Yet she hadn't really lied. She did have the beginnings of a headache. Probably from drinking that whisky so quickly. She also realised that by tomorrow night her tension would be beyond a joke after spending all day in Blake's company. He would expect her to have breakfast with him, swim with him, go to the races with him, possibly go out to dinner afterwards with friends, then come home and sleep with him. Better she get over the sex hurdle tonight or it might grow too daunting for her to handle.

'Blake...'

'Yes?'

'Just because I have a headache it doesn't mean you can't—um—I wouldn't mind. Really I wouldn't.'

The curl of his top lip showed distaste at her offer. 'Well, *I* would. I'm not so desperate as to force myself on my wife when she's unwell.'

'You wouldn't be forcing yourself on me, Blake,' she said huskily.

'Wouldn't I?' His eyes narrowed as they scanned her strained face.

She couldn't help it. She looked away, for fear of all he might see.

'For pity's sake, let's not make a song and dance about a bit of sex,' he said with offhand brusqueness. 'Tomorrow night will serve just as well. I'm probably more tired than I thought tonight, anyway.'

Whirling away, he was in the process of stalking off down the hallway towards his own room when he stopped abruptly and turned to face a still frozen Juliana.

'One thing before I forget,' he said sharply. 'The door leading in from the garages was unlocked when I got home. That's being a little careless, considering the level of break-ins in this neighbourhood.'

His accusatory tone flustered her. 'I don't usually forget,' she defended, 'but the telephone was ringing as I was letting myself in and it distracted me.'

'I see. Well, try to remember in future. A woman alone is very vulnerable. I would hate to see anything happen to you, Juliana. You're very important to me, you know. Well, goodnight again.'

Juliana stared after his departing figure.

No, I *don't* know! she thought with sudden venom.

I must have been mad to go into a marriage like this, she agonised. Simply mad! Whatever possessed me to accept Blake's cold-blooded proposal that night?

It couldn't have really been his money. Money would never have induced me to put my self-respect on the line like this. It must have been love. I must have been in love with Blake all along!

CHAPTER FOUR

JULIANA blinked amazement at this new line of thought. Shaking her head, she moved slowly into the bedroom, shutting the door behind her. How could she have loved Blake all along without knowing it? It seemed impossible.

Sighing her frustration, she moved over to the brass bed, tossed off her dressing-gown and climbed in between the cool crisp sheets. The pillows welcomed her by now woolly head. Maybe if she could just sleep, things would be clearer in the morning.

Sleep, however, eluded her. It was as though, once this idea had implanted itself in her mind, it refused to let go. She found herself reliving key events in her relationship with Blake, trying to see them through more mature and less emotion-charged eyes.

Finally, Juliana had to accept that a romantic love, as opposed to a platonic love, *might* have lain dormant within her without her knowing it. Blake had come along in her life when she'd been only a little girl, a very lonely little girl. In the beginning, he'd been the father she'd never known; the big brother she'd never had; the close friend she'd always craved.

These roles had clouded the main role a handsome young man might have eventually played for a young girl once she reached puberty: that of boyfriend and lover. But by then the difference in their backgrounds had erected other barriers that made such a relationship undesirable and unwise.

Appreciating these barriers far better than her younger self, Blake kept his distance once Juliana started to grow up, thereby stunting the growth of any unconscious hopes and dreams she had probably been harbouring about him. After all, if she hadn't been secretly attracted to Blake, why had she been so fiercely jealous of his many girlfriends?

Juliana only had to look at the incident after her graduation ball to realise something could easily have flared between them that night if she'd allowed it to. *She* had called a halt to Blake's attempted seduction, put off by the fact that his interest in her was only alcohol-inspired lust. Which it undoubtedly was.

Her own sexual responses that night could not be so easily explained away.

Looking back, Juliana suspected that if she'd given in to those responses back then her love for Blake might have exploded from its platonic-coated shell. But where would that have got her at sixteen? Blake certainly wouldn't have felt impelled to marry her. He simply would have toyed with her, as he'd toyed with all his other girlfriends. She would have been dropped eventually. No doubt about it.

Other questions popped into her mind as she mused about her past behaviour. Why had she guarded her virginity so maniacally all those years, only to throw it away with a kind of despairing indifference the night she heard Blake had become engaged to another woman? And why choose that particular night finally to say yes to Owen's repeated proposals of marriage, if not because she subconsciously accepted that Blake was no longer a possible husband?

Blake...

Her secret hero. Her dream man. Her Prince Charming.

Yet he was hardly a Prince Charming.

Oh, maybe he had been once, before life tainted and warped his judgement of people and relationships. There'd been a kindness, an open-hearted generosity in the adolescent Blake that had drawn Juliana to him. The adult Blake, however, was ruled by a world-weary cynicism, not to mention a wariness of love, that made him capable of all sorts of things.

Juliana could still recall her shock when he'd proposed to her that night. There again, it had been a night of many shocks...

Owen had been the instigator of the first. They'd been about to go out on a dinner-date on the eve of her twenty-sixth birthday. She'd been running late because she'd been kept back at work to finish some problem or other. She remembered she had been putting the last touches to her appearance when Owen had come into her bedroom, watching her in silence while she applied some burgundy lip gloss that exactly matched her burgundy crêpe dress.

She'd smiled at him over her shoulder as she put in her long dangling gold earrings. It was then that he'd come out with it.

'You do realise you won't be working after we're married, Juliana.'

Her hand froze on the last earring. She hoped she'd heard wrong. Frowning, she forced the last earring in then turned slowly to face her fiancé. 'I do realise I can't stay on at Hawthorne Bros once I'm your wife, Owen,' she agreed. 'That's company policy. But I intend finding another job.'

'No.'

'What do you mean, no?'

'I mean no, you won't be getting another job.'

She could not believe her ears. Owen, playing the controlling husband? If he knew her at all, he would know that was anathema to her.

His handsome face carried an appeasing smile as he came forward to take her in his arms. 'I want you free to travel with me, Juliana,' he said silkily. 'How can we just pack up and go off at will if you're tied down to a job?'

Juliana immediately felt a sense of panic take hold deep within her. She struggled against the awful suspicion that her engagement to this man was one big mistake. 'I have no objection to an extended honeymoon,' she compromised, 'but I can't envisage my life without my own job and my own money.'

'But you'll have all the money you want,' he argued softly. 'I'll open a special bank account for you to cover all your needs. You won't find me lacking in generosity, Juliana. You'll be kept in the manner to which I'm sure you'll quickly become accustomed.'

Juliana only heard one word. *Kept.*

She drew back to stare up at the man she'd thought she loved, thought she wanted to marry.

'I doubt I'd ever get accustomed to being *kept*,' she said shakily.

His laughter was dry. 'Come now, Juliana. You can't tell me you want to go on working in a dreary office when you can live the high life. Just think! You won't have to get up till lunchtime if you don't want to.'

'But I *hate* sleeping in!' she protested, further warning bells going off in her brain.

'That's because you're not used to it. Poor darling, you've had to work so hard just to make ends meet. It will be my pleasure to spoil you. All you have to do in return is be my loving wife. Now that won't be so hard, will it?'

He kissed her full on the mouth, his wet tongue demanding entry. Normally, Juliana didn't mind Owen's kisses. She usually found his ardour comforting, the body contact soothing the deep loneliness within her. Suddenly she found him cloying in the extreme.

Suppressing a shudder, she allowed him a few brief moments before pulling her mouth away, horrified at the growing repulsion within her heart and body. With an apologetic grimace, she eased herself out of his hold. 'Please, Owen, I can't think when you're doing that, and I need to talk to you.'

'I can't think when I'm doing that either,' came his desire-thickened reply. 'I'm mad about you, Juliana. You must know that.'

She stared at him. Yes, she did. But was madness love? And what of her own feelings? It was hard to keep telling herself she was in love with the man when his kiss just now had repelled her so. Just thinking about going to bed with him again made her feel sick to the stomach.

There was no doubt about it. She could not go through with this marriage.

'I won't ever give up working,' she said firmly. 'It's who I am.'

Owen's face showed exasperation. 'Who you are? What kind of crap is that? You're Juliana, my fiancée, soon to be my wife!'

'I don't think so...' Looking down, she began removing the diamond engagement-ring from her finger. 'I...I'm sorry, Owen,' she said as she held it out to him.

He stared down at her outstretched hand. 'You must be joking.'

'Unfortunately, no. But surely you can see that marriage between us wouldn't work. We just don't want the same things in life. It's best we found that out now, before it was too late. Please, Owen...take the ring.'

He backhanded her fingers with a vicious slap, sending the ring flying across the room. 'Keep the bloody thing!' he snarled. 'You might need it to pawn when you're starving. And you will be, honey, if you stay in this town. Come Monday you won't have a job, a reference, or a reputation. You'll find life can be pretty tough on the bastard daughter of a crummy cook who hasn't the brains to know what side her bread's buttered on. You stupid bitch! You could have had it all! But what can you expect from the gutter class? I should have listened to my friends.'

He stormed out of the flat, leaving Juliana to stare, pale-faced and wide-eyed, after him. Shock was her first reaction, for she had never seen that side of Owen before, never dreamt he could be so violent and vengeful.

But shock was soon replaced by a crippling anxiety. Owen had the wealth and power to do what he threatened. She was a woman alone in the world with no one to turn to, no one to help her. No one except . . .

'Blake,' she whispered aloud.

She didn't stop to think if he would be home. She simply called a taxi and went over to the Preston house and rang the front doorbell. Blake's new cook-housekeeper answered, a dour widow named Mrs Dawson.

'Yes?' the woman asked suspiciously before recognising Juliana. 'Oh, it's you, Miss Mason.' Juliana had met Mrs Dawson when she'd come over to remove her mother's effects a few weeks before. Not that there had been a lot. Some clothes and jewellery. A few ornaments and photographs. Not much to represent a whole life. When Juliana had expressed as much to Blake that weekend, he'd said that *she* was her mother's legacy to the world.

'Lily was very proud of you, Juliana,' were his parting words that day.

Juliana closed her eyes for a second. Oh, Mum, I wish you were still alive. I need you, need your love and support. I'm frightened.

'Is there something I can do for you, Miss Mason?' the housekeeper asked.

'I have to speak to Blake. Is he home?'

'I'm afraid not. Would you like to leave a message?'

What possible message could she leave? Blake, I've jilted Owen and he's going to take revenge by blackening my name and making sure I can't get a decent job in Melbourne?

You didn't put such a message in the hands of a stranger.

'I need to see him personally. Can I wait, do you think? Will he be coming home tonight?'

Mrs Dawson looked dubious. 'He might be very late...'

'I don't mind. I really need to see him. It's a matter of life and death.'

Mrs Dawson sniffed down her not inconsiderable nose. 'Well, I suppose you can wait, if you must.'

'I must.'

'Come into the family-room then. There's a television there. I was about to watch the Friday night movie.'

Mrs Dawson retired at ten-thirty after the movie finished, an incomprehensible thriller that had about as much suspense as a parliamentary sitting. Not that Juliana was in a fit state to view television. Still, she had to do something while she awaited Blake's return. She was sitting there blankly watching the screen around eleven-thirty when she heard a car rumble into the garages.

Blake was home.

Jumping to her feet, she raced into the kitchen, where she practically collided with him on his way through.

'Juliana!' He smiled for second when he first realised whom he'd run into. But then a frown claimed his smile. 'What on earth are you doing here at this hour?'

'Waiting for you.'

'But why?'

'I ... I need help.'

'What kind of help?'

'It's hard to explain. Do you think I could make us both a cup of coffee while I tell you? This could take some time ...'

'To hell with coffee. Let's have a real drink. I'm in dire need. Follow me.'

'What's wrong with *you*?' she asked as she hurried after him into what had once been his father's study. It was not a room she'd been in often, certainly not since it had been redecorated. Gone was the old-world stuffy look, replaced by sleek modern lines to match its new occupant. The colours were predominantly grey and black, the curtains a dark red. Blake's black trousers and grey silk shirt blended perfectly.

He shot her a rueful glance from behind the built-in corner bar. 'I doubt you'd be interested. You'd only say it serves me right, that rich bastards like myself deserve all we get. Or has your attitude to rich bastards changed since you got engaged to the honourable Owen Hawthorne?'

Sighing, Juliana lowered herself into a squishy black leather armchair. 'Not exactly.' Her voice reeked with an acid bitterness. 'If anything, it's got worse.'

Blake's eyebrows shot up. 'I take it all is not well in lovers' land?

'I'm going to flush his engagement-ring down the toilet when I get home! After I've found it, that is.'

Blake laughed. 'I take it you've had a little spat?'

'Hardly little. And it's not a laughing matter, Blake. The man's threatening to strip me of my job and my reputation. He says I won't ever get a decent position in Melbourne again.'

'Good God, Juliana, whatever did you do? Have you been playing around behind his back or something?'

Juliana shot Blake a savage look. 'Is that what you think of me? That I'm no better than a two-timing tramp?'

His shrug was irritatingly nonchalant. 'I think you're a very beautiful, ambitious young woman who always said she'd marry a millionaire. Can I be blamed for thinking that love might not have come into the arrangement, and that you might have become a fraction bored with Owen's perfor-mance in bed? I've heard rumours that he wouldn't get into the *Guinness Book of Records* as the world's greatest lover.'

Juliana wished she could have stopped the fierce blush coming to her cheeks. She'd often thought that Owen wasn't the most skilful of lovers. He was much too fast. But, considering her own tendency to be less than passionate in bed, she had brushed aside any concern over the matter. She'd already come to the conclusion that sex was overrated, anyway.

Still, Blake's assumption that a man's ineptness in bed excused faithlessness annoyed her. As did his assumption that she was little more than a cold-blooded gold-digger.

'I'll have you know that I am not into the casual bed-hopping your lot seem to indulge in,' she countered sharply. 'I also would not dream of being unfaithful to the man I was engaged to. To me, an engagement is as serious a commitment as marriage. When I marry, it will be for life! That's why I broke my engagement. *I*, not Owen. I knew it wouldn't work out.'

'Why wouldn't it work out?' Blake came forward with a couple of glasses filled with whisky and ice. He pressed one into her hands and sat in a chair adjacent to her, watching her face as she struggled to find the right words.

'I...I...'

'Didn't you love him?' came the probing query.

Juliana sighed. 'I *thought* I did...'

'But you realised you didn't.'

'Yes.'

'When?'

'When he demanded I give up work after we were married.'

Blake laughed. 'Stupid man. That would have been the kiss of death with you. Clearly he doesn't know you very well.'

Juliana couldn't help it. She laughed too. But then she sobered. 'Whatever am I going to do, Blake?'

'It's quite simple, really, if you're prepared to put aside the romantic notion of marrying for love.'

She stared over at him. 'I'm not sure what you're getting at. I'm not going to change my mind and marry Owen. Even if I loved him, I wouldn't marry a man who demanded I give up everything for him. I don't believe in that type of love.'

'Believe me, neither do I,' Blake returned drily. 'But I'm not suggesting you still marry Hawthorne. I'm suggesting you marry me.'

Juliana was lost for words. For a second, a strange elation swept through her. Till she remembered one crucial factor. 'But you're already engaged!' she burst out.

'Actually, no... I'm not. I broke it off tonight. That's why I was home early.'

'But... but *why*?'

His expression was deadpan. 'Would you believe I found out tonight that Virginia was planning to do what Owen wanted you to do?'

'What? Give up her job after the wedding?'

His smile held no humour as he nodded. 'Perverse, isn't it?'

She could think of nothing to say. Knowing Blake as she did, she knew that he would shrink from having a wife staying home and devoting herself entirely to him.

'Did... did you love her?' she asked at last, the question sticking in her throat for some reason.

He shrugged. 'What's love? I enjoyed making love to her. I also thought she would make a good mother. I want children, Juliana.'

'And Virginia didn't?'

'Not for donkey's ages. That was the straw that broke this camel's back.'

'I . . . I see.'

'I thought you would. You know me as well as I know you. So what do you say? If you marry me, Juliana, you won't have to worry about Owen Hawthorne's threats. I'll make sure they come to nothing. I'll also make sure you get a really good job, something even more satisfying than you have at the moment.'

Juliana could only shake her head. 'Blake, this is crazy!' Yet, crazy as it was, she could not deny she felt quite excited by the idea.

'Why is it crazy? You're everything I could possibly want in a wife—beautiful, intelligent, independent. And you'd make a good mother too. You *want* children, don't you?'

'Yes, of course.'

'I thought so. You had a good example of maternal love.'

'Aren't you worried that if I said yes I might be marrying you for your money?'

He smiled. 'Not at all. In fact, it would please me if that were the case.'

'Blake!'

'You don't honestly think I want you madly in love with me, do you?' he retorted curtly. 'I need that kind of marriage like I need a hole in the head. It will be quite enough if you like and respect me as much as I've always liked and respected you.'

She flushed with pleasure at his words. But the pleasure was tinged with worry. 'But . . . but what about sex?'

'What about it?'

'I . . . I don't think I'm very good at it.'

His eyebrows shot up. 'I find that hard to believe.'

She sighed. 'Well, believe me, it's true.'

'The girl I kissed on her graduation night was not even remotely frigid. You let me worry about the sex, Juliana. So what do you say? Will you marry me?'

Her lips remained pressed tightly together, even though the temptation to just say yes was quite strong.

'Think of the alternative,' he argued softly. 'No job; no reputation; no future. As my wife, you'll hold a position of power and privilege in this town. No one will turn their nose up at you, believe me. They'll kowtow and grovel. And no daughter of ours will ever have to wear a second-hand gown to her graduation . . .'

Was it this last incisively timed remark that made up her mind for her?

Juliana had thought so at the time; had thought her decision to marry Blake had been one of bitter practicality.

Now she knew different.

She'd wanted to marry Blake all along, loved him all along. But she would never have what she really wanted: his love in return.

'Oh, Blake . . . Blake,' she cried, and turned to bury her face into the pillow.

CHAPTER FIVE

'MORNING.' Blake breezed into the kitchen dressed far too sexily in a pair of tight stone-washed jeans and a blue windcheater the exact colour of his eyes. His thick tawny hair, Juliana noted, was still darkly damp from the shower, and trying to curl. It always did that when it was going to rain.

'Morning,' she returned crisply, and lowered her eyes again to the frying-pan, a silent groan echoing a painful acceptance that her sexual awareness of Blake had only increased overnight, as she'd feared it would. As though in readiness for this frustrating event, she herself was wearing a loosely fitting tracksuit in a very nondescript grey flannel.

Blake perched up on one of the kitchen stools. 'How are you feeling this morning?' he asked. 'Better?'

'Much better, thank you.'

Normally, Juliana liked Saturday breakfast, liked the relaxed informality of Blake chatting away to her while she performed her one cooking chore of the week. Today, she was far from relaxed.

'You don't look all that great,' he remarked.

Juliana gave him a dry look. 'I'm fine. Stop fussing. If I did that to you, you'd give me short shrift.'

He laughed. 'So I would. But maybe you should have a nap this afternoon. You've got dark rings under your eyes.'

'Aren't we supposed to be going to go to the races this afternoon?'

'Nope. Rain's forecast. I can't bear the races in the rain. Besides, I thought two trips to Flemington in one week might be too much for you. I know you're not *that* keen. Or have you forgotten what next week is?'

Juliana groaned out loud as she remembered it was the first week in November, Melbourne Cup week. Usually she avoided the famous spring racing carnival, because the crowds were horrendous, but the company she worked for, Femme Fatale Cosmetics, had booked one of the promotional marquees for Oaks Day on the Thursday—Ladies' Day. In her position as public relations officer, she would be obliged to go.

'Damn,' she muttered. 'I'll have to buy a new outfit, hat and all. Are you coming with me on the Thursday? You weren't sure when I told you about it before.'

'Sorry. Can't. From what Stewart told me last night, the Sydney branch could do with a good shake-up. I'm going to fly up there on Monday and stay the week.'

The news that Blake was going away so soon after his return did not depress Juliana as much as it would have done a day ago. She almost felt relieved. She certainly looked up at her husband with a brightening smile on her face. 'That's all right. I'll find someone else to go with me.'

She was startled by Blake's answering scowl. 'Well, you don't have to sound so happy about it. I thought you liked my company.'

'I *do*!'

'Do you? I'm beginning to wonder after last night.'

Juliana was taken aback—and somewhat annoyed—by his nasty tone. It was so unjustified. 'Blake, I had a headache. And, if you remember correctly, I didn't refuse to sleep with you. You *chose* not to.'

'Out of consideration for you,' he pointed out testily.

'Out of deference to your male ego, more likely!' she shot back. 'You don't consider *me*, Blake. You only ever consider *yourself*!'

For a long moment, they stared at each other, both angry, yet shocked as well. Blake especially. Juliana had never spoken to him like this before, had never accused him of callous selfishness.

His expression was unlike any Juliana had ever seen on Blake. He was pale. Shaken. Yet simmering with a barely held fury. 'My dear Juliana,' he said, his low monotone evidence of the difficulty he was having in containing his temper. 'You knew full well the sort of man I was when you married me. I *am* selfish, I admit it. But not in a sexual sense. If I were a selfish lover, I would have spent the night with you anyway, and to hell with your feelings!'

'You *never* spend the night with me,' she flung back resentfully. 'And it's *often* to hell with my feelings!'

He glared at her, his blue eyes getting colder by the second. The smell of burning bacon was filling the kitchen but both of them ignored it, each equally intent on venting their own anger.

'If by that remark you're saying I *don't* always satisfy you in a sexual sense, then you're the best darned faker in the business! Even on our wedding night, when you were as nervous as a kitten, I managed to do the right thing by you. If that wasn't my considering your feelings then I don't know what it was!'

Juliana flushed guiltily as she recalled her wedding night. Blake was right. That could have been a disaster, she'd been so nervous and uptight.

They hadn't gone away for a honeymoon after their simple register office ceremony; Blake had not wanted a big white wedding or any fuss. She had agreed at the time, since she had still been somewhat embarrassed over the speed of their marriage, a mere month after Blake had proposed.

Yet during that month not once had Blake touched her in an intimate or sexual manner, except for a couple of quick goodnight kisses. Juliana found herself on her wedding-day wishing that he had, so that the night ahead didn't loom as such unknown territory. Questions kept flashing through her mind all day. Would she be as hopeless as she had been with Owen in bed? Would she find herself tensing up as she always did once her clothes were removed? Would she always be left feeling inadequate and guilty?

She was an intelligent woman and knew that all the blame could not be put on Owen for her failure to find fulfilment on the occasions when she'd had sex with him. When she'd told Blake she wasn't any good at sex, she had meant it.

So when the time had come to undress, that first night, she'd been almost in a state of frozen panic. Blake had recognised that she was a cot-case, and in deference to her nerves—or so she had thought at the time—had told her to shower and pop into her own bed and turn out the light.

She had done what he suggested, but had still been literally shaking when he'd finally come into the room and slipped between the sheets.

'You're naked!' she gasped.

'And you're not,' was his dry reply.

'Yes, well, I . . . I . . .'

'Hush,' he said, and gathered her close. 'We'll just talk till you stop shaking.'

'T-talk?'

'Yes, talk. You were always pretty good at talking. Maybe if we start with something you *are* good at we'll get your confidence up and things can progress from there.'

'I wouldn't b-bet on it if I w-were you,' she returned, her teeth chattering.

'We'll see, honey, we'll see. So tell me about your new job. Do you like working in public relations rather than marketing?'

And that was how he went on, asking her question after question till her mind was totally distracted from the sex that was to come. It was only later that she realised that somewhere along the line he had subtly started touching her, stroking her, kissing her. First on her shoulder, then her neck, her ear, her cheek, her forehead, her nose, and finally...her mouth.

It was at that point that the question-and-answer technique had given way to a more direct line of action. Not that Blake had turned animal or anything. He'd remained patient and gentle, skilfully removing her nightwear without frightening her, after which he'd showed her that passion did not necessarily have to be either savage or wild. It could be slow-building and sweet. Blake whispered soft, tender endearments to her while he caressed her breasts and kissed her mouth, telling her she had a beautiful body and that he wanted to lose himself in it.

Which he eventually did. But not roughly, and certainly not quickly. She remembered how surprised she'd felt at first when it had looked as if he would never stop. Not that it wasn't pleasant. It was. No...*more* than pleasant. It was quite exciting, causing her heart to race and an alien heat to invade every corner of her body.

She'd felt vaguely embarrassed by her responses, the way her lips fell apart to let escape her rapid panting, the way her body started arching up to meet Blake's powerfully deep surges. And then ... Oh, God, then she'd felt as if everything was squeezing so tightly inside her. She'd cried out in a type of startled shock, but soon her cry had turned to a sensuous gasp followed by an even, shaming moan, then finally to a long, contented, shuddering sigh.

Juliana flushed again at the memory of that night, and all the nights since when she'd moaned beneath Blake's skilful hands.

But moans could mean many different things. Physical satisfaction perhaps, but also pain, as well as emotional torment. Would she moan a different type of moan tonight?

'You can't deny that I satisfy you in bed, Juliana,' Blake reiterated with some asperity.

'There are many types of satisfaction,' she muttered, truthfully but perhaps unwisely.

His glare was harsh. 'Meaning?'

Juliana finally realised that she had crossed over into very dangerous territory with this argument.

She shook her head and turned her attention to the already charred bacon. 'I'll have to cook some more. This is ruined.'

'Don't brush me off, damn you!'

Juliana stared up at Blake's now standing figure. The muscles in his face were taut, his jaw squared angrily, his fists clenched on the counter-top. God, he looked as if he wanted to hit her.

She scooped in a deep, steadying breath, letting it out slowly. 'I'm not brushing you off. You're right and I'm wrong. You're a wonderful lover and you always satisfy me, OK?'

'No, it's not OK. You're obviously disgruntled about something but won't come out with it!'

'It's nothing, Blake.'

'So you won't tell me.'

'There's nothing to tell!' she insisted.

'You're lying, Juliana. Something's troubling you and you don't have enough confidence—or *guts*—to tell me.'

She sighed. 'Don't make a mountain out of a molehill, Blake. It's nothing. Honestly. I've just been out of sorts lately, that's all. Please sit back down and I'll cook us some more breakfast.'

For a few startling moments she thought he was going to stalk out of the room. It would have been a most uncharacteristic gesture on Blake's part. He was not given to violent moods, or fits of temper. A dry sarcasm was the furthest he went in expressing disapproval or anger.

Juliana watched with a measure of astonishment as he battled with his emotions. Briefly it looked as if he *was* going to act like a typically infuriated spouse.

But then the old Blake resurfaced and he shrugged offhandedly, the tense lines in his face melting away. 'I guess I'm not used to your being temperamental,' he said with wry relief in his voice.

Juliana's fingers tightened around the plastic scoop she was holding, lest she lash out at him with it. If only he would show her for once that he really cared about her. If only he *would* storm out of the room, or just lose his temper. Anything would be better than this detached persona he hid behind all the time.

But she said nothing, did nothing, merely went on with cooking some more breakfast, letting Blake move the conversation round to less threatening topics. Yet all the while, underneath, she remained troubled. Where would all this end? How soon before she blew up again over some inconsequential matter, simply because she wanted more than Blake could give?

The problem seemed insurmountable. As much as she'd thought last night that she would do anything to save her marriage, Juliana now wasn't so sure. Maybe trying to save this marriage would prove too costly...

The telephone ringing towards the end of breakfast startled Juliana, making her jump up from her stool. Her nerves were obviously still on edge. Blake darted her an odd glance before reaching up to lift the receiver down from the wall. 'Yes?' he answered nondescriptly.

Nothing could be gleaned from Blake's end of the conversation, either who was calling or what it was all about.

'Hi, there... Really? That's thoughtful of you... Yes, we would... Send them over in a taxi... I'll pay for it... Thanks again... Yes, we will... Bye.'

'What was that all about?' she asked as he hung up.

'Jack Marsden had tickets for himself and Gloria to see *Phantom of the Opera* tonight but they can't go. Gloria's mother's ill and they have to visit her this weekend. He knows how much you like the show so he immediately thought we might like to go. He's sending the tickets over in a taxi.'

'Oh, how marvellous!' Juliana exclaimed, instantly excited despite the events of the morning. She'd seen the show for the first time earlier that year and had been dying to go again, but all the good seats were booked out months in advance.

'But how did he know I liked the show?' she asked, and started to clear up.

'I guess I must have mentioned it to him after we went last time, and, being the canny businessman that he is, he remembered. Jack wants me to invest some money in his construction firm. He'd go and buy tickets on the black market if he thought it would get him in my good books.'

Juliana could not help a sad little sigh. 'Why do you have to be such a cynic?'

'A realist, Juliana, not a cynic.'

'I can't see the difference.'

A dark cloud marred his beautiful blue eyes as he looked at her. 'You know, Juliana, I always thought you liked me.'

'Don't be silly, Blake, I *do* like you.'

'But not my so-called cynicism.'

'That's right.'

There was a short, sharp silence. Juliana bent to the task of clearing up.

'It will be our first anniversary in two months,' he resumed abruptly.

She looked up, forcing a smile to her lips. 'Yes, it will be. Why do you mention it?'

'I thought I might remind you of the agreement we made before we were married that if after the first year we thought our marriage wasn't working out, or if either of us did something foolish like fall in love with someone else, then we would call it quits.'

Juliana swallowed. She hoped she didn't look as sick as she felt. 'What . . . what are you trying to say? *Have* you fallen in love with someone else?'

His expression was startled. 'Don't be ridiculous. Love and I had a parting of the ways years ago. Good God, what a ghastly idea!'

'Then what *are* you trying to say?'

'I'm not exactly sure. I did think you were happy. But last night, and this morning...' He shrugged, clearly confused by the situation.

Yet his confusion touched Juliana. She wanted to stop what she was doing, take him in her arms, hug him, tell him she would never leave him.

Of course she couldn't do that. All she could do was try to verbally reassure him that she *was* happy, that she would *never* leave him. But before she could say a single word, he swept on, mocking in his self-reproach.

'Hell, what am I doing, asking you for reassurance like an insecure child, just because you're in a bit of a mood? I'm quite sure that if you wanted out of this marriage you'd tell me. You've always been as straight as a die.' His wry grin dismissed any lingering irritation. 'So! What are we going to do for the rest of the day?'

Juliana felt quite annoyed with him. There he'd been, about to lock horns with real emotions, real feelings, however confusing they might be. And what had he done? Once again darted behind that impenetrable shield, the one that closed tight around his heart, the one that shut out anything that could make him seem vulnerable in any way.

'I don't know about you,' she returned sharply 'but I have to go shopping for clothes. Then I have to get my hair trimmed, after which I've been ordered to take a nap, since I have horrible dark rings under my eyes. But, since *you* have nothing to do, you can start by putting these dishes in the dishwasher!'

And with that she dropped everything, spun round and stalked from the kitchen, uncaring that Blake was gaping after her with his mouth open and blue eyes blinking wide.

CHAPTER SIX

JULIANA returned to the house from her shopping and hairdressing expedition as late as she possibly could, informing Mrs Dawson on the way through that she would have a small tray of toasted sandwiches in her room rather than a sit-down meal that night.

'What about Mr Preston?' the housekeeper asked. 'What will he be having?'

Juliana stopped and frowned. 'Hasn't he said anything to you about our going out to see *The Phantom of the Opera* tonight?'

'Not a word,' the woman sniffed. 'He left shortly after I arrived back this morning. I think he went out to play golf, since he took his golf-clubs with him.'

'Golf? In the rain?'

'Rain doesn't bother a man if he wants to play golf,' Mrs Dawson humphed. 'My Fred used to play all weekend, come rain, hail or shine. Can't see the attraction myself. A lot of walking and very little playing.'

'I couldn't agree more,' Juliana said with a small smile. She imagined poor Fred was only too glad to be out of the house and away from his bossy wife.

Suddenly, and quite unexpectedly, the other woman smiled too, showing good teeth behind her

thin lips and quite attractive dimples in her cheeks.
For once Mrs Dawson looked the fifty-five she was
rather than a sour sixty-five. Then she did something else that astounded Juliana. She gave her a
compliment. 'Your hair looks good that length, Mrs
Preston.'

'Oh, do you think so?'

Juliana hadn't been too pleased with the hair-
dresser when she'd cut off much more than her
usual one-inch trim, leaving it swinging just on her
shoulders rather than resting down on her shoulder-
blades. It wouldn't have happened if she hadn't
been so distracted over Blake, and while all the girls
in the salon had said it suited her she hadn't been
too sure. Yet here was Mrs Dawson actually smiling
at her and agreeing with them. In that case, it had
to be true.

'It's still long enough to put up if you want to,'
the housekeeper advised her with her usual
practicality.

'Yes, I suppose so. I hope Blake likes it.'

'I doubt Mr Preston will even notice. Men don't
notice such things about their wives. They only
notice on *other* ladies.'

Juliana was inclined to agree with her. Still, the
caustic comment underlined the fact that maybe
dear old Fred had been doing a little more than
playing golf during his lifetime. 'He certainly won't
notice tonight, since I'm going to put it up.'

'When would you like me to bring up your tray,
Mrs Preston?' the housekeeper asked with yet
another astonishing smile.

Juliana found it hard to get used to the house-keeper's unexpected warmth, but she was not about to lose the opportunity to become friendly. The woman's stiff attitude towards her had been hard to live with. 'Not till six,' Juliana said. 'Oh, and Mrs Dawson . . .'

'Yes?'

'Please call me Juliana.'

The housekeeper was taken aback, yet clearly pleased. *Perhaps she never disliked me at all*, Juliana decided. *Maybe Blake insisted when he employed her that she keep her distance. That would be just like him.*

This last idea was almost confirmed by the woman's saying warily, 'But . . . but what about Mr Preston?'

'You can call *him* anything you darned well like,' Juliana said firmly. 'But in future *I* will only answer to Juliana.'

'In that case, you'd better call me Susanne.'

'Susanne. What a lovely name!' Juliana beamed. 'But enough of this girl-talk; I'd better get a move on if I'm to be ready on time.'

'Anything I can do to help? Any ironing?' Susanne Dawson nodded towards the parcels Juliana was carrying.

'No, these aren't for tonight. They're for Ladies Day at the races next Thursday. I'm going to wear my green velvet tonight.'

'Ah, that's a lovely dress. But you're right, it would look better with your hair up. Then everyone can see the pretty sweetheart neckline. Better shake a leg then, Mrs——' She broke off with a wry chuckle. 'Better hurry, Juliana. I'll be up on the dot of six with a tray.'

Juliana laughed as she raced up the stairs. But, as she swept into her bedroom and looked at that bed again, any feelings of buoyancy faded. Not even the prospect of seeing her favourite musical in a couple of hours could revive her spirits. All she could think about was afterwards ...

'You're looking lovely tonight, Juliana,' Blake said blandly on the way to the theatre in a taxi.

She slanted a long, thoughtful look his way. He was sitting there, staring away from her through the passenger window to his right, casually resplendent in pale cream trousers and a shirt, a blue-grey blazer lending the outfit a slightly nautical look.

'Thank you,' she returned just as non-committally, thinking to herself how like Blake it was to come home shortly after she had that afternoon and not say a word about the morning's altercation; how like him not to question her arrangements about that night's meal; how *very* like him to compliment her appearance without really looking at her.

'Susanne thinks this colour looks well on me,' she added with a perversely mischievous smile. For she knew her remark would draw a reaction.

His head turned, his fair hair glinting as they passed under a bright street-light. 'Susanne? Who's Susanne?'

'Our housekeeper.'

He lifted a single eyebrow. 'Since when have you two been on first-name basis?'

'Since today.'

'And what brought that on? You know I like to keep my employees at arm's length.'

'Yes. But I don't.'

He stared at her for a few seconds. 'What in God's name is bugging you, Juliana? This can hardly be some sort of women's liberation kick, since you'd have to be the most liberated woman I know. I don't make you answer to me for anything.'

'Good,' she snapped. 'Then I don't have to explain why I've chosen to call Mrs Dawson by her first name, do I?'

She saw the anger well up in his eyes and revelled in it. Go on, she urged in silent desperation. Lose your temper with me, right here in this taxi, in front of a stranger. *Do it*!

He sucked in a ragged breath. His blue eyes glittered dangerously. His fists were clenched tightly by his side.

But, in the end, he didn't lose his temper. Taking a few moments to control himself, he eventually presented to her a totally composed face. Or was it a façade? Juliana had to admit that a muscle still twitched in his cheek. Was that evidence of the intensity of the struggle that was going on inside him? Or simply a sign of male anger that she should have put him in such an invidious position? Juliana knew Blake would be hating this.

'No,' he said in a low, deadly voice. 'You don't. Now if you don't mind I would like to terminate this conversation. *Right now*,' he bit out under his breath. 'I can't abide couples who make scenes in public.'

Juliana knew when she had pushed an issue as far as she could. Besides, what had she hoped to achieve? Was this how her love for Blake was going to take voice from now on, by her trying to goad him into an emotional response, no matter what it was?

She sighed her depression at living life on such a tightrope.

'They're still working on the road outside the theatre,' the taxi driver said just then over his shoulder. 'But I'll get you as close as I can.'

There was an atmosphere of excitement before each performance of *Phantom of the Opera*, the musical that had already become legendary, and in a way the traffic bedlam outside the old Princess Theatre only added to that air of excitement. Juliana found herself caught up in it the moment she climbed out of the taxi. People were pouring out of tour buses; others were being dropped off by car and taxi; still more simply walked up from where they'd either parked or alighted from trams.

'Do you want to fight your way through for a drink at the bar,' Blake asked as they made their way slowly towards the crowded entrance, 'or shall we go straight to our seats?'

'I suppose we might as well head for our seats,' she said with a frowning glance at the even more crowded bar on the left. Really, both the foyer and the bar were far too small, but it was the only theatre in Melbourne—in Australia for that matter—that had the kind of stage that could accommodate such a show as *Phantom*. It also brought an enormous amount of tourist trade to

Melbourne, so Juliana supposed the locals couldn't complain. Still, she would have liked a drink, a fact which Blake must have noted.

'I'll get you a glass of champagne at half-time,' he promised.

The show was as marvellous as it had been the first time Juliana had seen it, even though there had been some changes of cast since then. When the lights came on for the interval she gave a huge sigh of ragged pleasure.

'Isn't it a wonderful show?' she said. 'Spectacular and stirring and oh, so emotional. You can't help feeling sorry for the Phantom; he does love Christine so...'

Blake turned to her with a sardonic smile on his face. 'I didn't realise you were such a romantic, Juliana. The man's a maniac and a murderer. My sympathies go to Raoul, not to mention the theatre owners.'

'Yours would,' she muttered.

His chuckle was dark. 'Because I'm an unfeeling bastard, or a businessman?'

'Aren't they one and the same?'

Juliana saw his eyes narrow with a flash of anger, but then he stood up to glance around the rapidly emptying seats. 'If I don't head for the bar post-haste I won't be back before the curtain goes up for the second half. Do you want to go to the Ladies'?'

'No. I'll just sit here.'

'OK.'

Juliana sighed as she watched him slip lithely through the groups of departing people. No doubt he would still get served fairly quickly. Blake had that effect on waiters and barmen.

She was sitting there, feeling unhappy with herself for the way she kept making inflammatory remarks to Blake, when the sounds of merriment behind her drew her attention. Looking back over her shoulder, she saw that a group of young people several rows back were laughing and joking in that rather loud manner young gentlemen and ladies often engaged in when they got together. Not that they were being loud enough to be offensive. The theatre was practically empty, anyway.

Juliana was simply amazed, however, to see that one of the young men was none other than Stewart Margin. She stared as Blake's normally prim and proper secretary began acting the goat with his friends, pulling faces and puffing out a non-existent bosom, clearly taking off the role of Carlotta in the show. When he suddenly noticed her staring back up at him, a dark flush of embarrassment stained his cheeks.

For a moment he didn't seem to know what to do. She too felt embarrassed for him, so she swung round and stared blankly ahead, doing her best to hide her slowly spreading smile. Who would have believed it? Stewart Margin was human after all! In a way it reminded Juliana of what happened that afternoon with Mrs Dawson. You could have knocked her over with a feather when Blake's housekeeper had smiled at her.

An unexpected tap on her shoulder had her spinning round in the narrow seat. Stewart was sitting in one of the empty seats behind her, looking worried but not altogether remorseful.

'Good evening, Mrs Preston,' he said somewhat stiffly, and somewhat in contrast to his performance of a few moments ago.

'Stewart...' Juliana could feel her lips twitching. Dear heaven, she was going to burst out laughing. She could feel it. In an effort to stop such a catastrophe, she bit her bottom lip.

'Is—um—Mr Preston with you?'

She nodded. It seemed the safest course.

'You—er—I mean ... I'm sorry if we were annoying you just then, Mrs Preston. I know we were a touch loud but we were only having a little bit of fun. I mean...you won't tell Mr Preston, will you? He thinks that I'm—er——' He sighed his frustration. 'The fact is, one must act in a certain manner in front of Mr Preston, or one doesn't get along with him, if you know what I mean ...'

Suddenly, any wish Juliana had to laugh dissolved into a longing to cry instead. She knew very well what Stewart meant. Very well indeed.

A sad little smile touched her lips as she reached out and patted the young man's hand. 'It's all right, Stewart. I fully understand. You weren't annoying me just now and I have no intention of telling Mr Preston. I suppose I was merely taken aback to see you—er—enjoying yourself so much.'

Now Stewart smiled. Grinned, actually. Juliana was surprised to see how attractive he was with his usually bland grey eyes twinkling. It came to her then that Blake's secretary would not be unpopular with women. 'You thought I was a stuffed shirt, I suppose,' he chuckled.

'You certainly give a good impression of one.'

His eyes flicked over her with such direct male appreciation that she was startled for a moment. 'And you, Mrs Preston, give a very good impression of a society wife. But I found out differently yesterday. You've got a heart, lady. Mr Preston is one lucky guy.'

Juliana flushed under the compliment. But along with the warm rush of pleasure came that longing to cry again. If only Blake *wanted* her heart...

'I'd better get back to my seat,' Stewart said when people started filing back into the row he was occupying. 'Thanks again, Mrs Preston. Look after yourself.'

She watched him make his way slowly along the row, wondering exactly how old he was. Twenty-six or -seven, perhaps? Younger than she'd always imagined. Before seeing him here tonight, she would have said thirty at least.

'Was that Stewart you were just talking to?'

Juliana swung back round to find Blake standing next to her, a tall glass of champagne in his hand.

'Er—um—yes—yes it was actually.' Dear lord, why did she have to sound so darned guilty?

As Blake handed the glass over to her she was stung by the coldness in his eyes. 'You two seemed to be having a very confidential little tête-à-tête. I had no idea you were so chummy.' He sat down, at last giving her some peace from the chill of his gaze. 'I also had no idea he would be here tonight. He certainly never mentioned it to me.'

'Well, why would he?' she defended. 'If you keep your employees at arm's length, they're not going to tell you about their private life, are they?'

'I suppose he tells *you* all about his private life, though,' he said silkily. 'Does he call you Juliana as well?'

'Don't be so ridiculous, Blake. You know he wouldn't dare.'

'Not in front of me, he wouldn't. But I've no idea what he might dare when I'm halfway across the world.'

Juliana's mouth dropped open as she turned to stare across at her stony-faced husband. 'My God, you're jealous!'

His top lip curled in open contempt of this suggestion, 'Now *you're* being ridiculous! I am not, however, a fool. And a fool I would be if I ever took a beautiful woman like you for granted. Now close your mouth and drink your champagne, Juliana. The curtain's about to go back up.'

It was to the credit of the show that within minutes Juliana forgot her emotional turmoil and became involved in the world of magical fantasy being played out on the stage. Though she would have been blind not to have seen the faint echo of her own situation in the storyline. The Phantom loved Christine to distraction, but it was to remain an unrequited love. Christine's heart belonged to another.

Blake's heart did not belong to another, Juliana conceded. It was simply incapable of loving her the way she wanted to be loved. Still . . . she shouldn't complain. He *did* care for her, in his own peculiar way. It would have to be enough.

They didn't spot Stewart in the crush of people after the show. Which was just as well, Juliana thought. Blake had been peeved by her chatting to his secretary. She didn't seriously believe he envisaged an affair between her and his secretary, but *nothing* was supposed to undermine the distance he liked to keep from those who worked for him. No doubt she'd already irritated the life out of him tonight by calling Mrs Dawson Susanne. Juliana was by nature a reserved person, but even she could see that Blake carried this obsession for insulation too far. Maybe it was time to quietly challenge it, to try to break it down somewhat. It wasn't a healthy attitude, she was sure of that.

Not tonight, however, she decided as they travelled home in a taxi in dead silence. She had done quite enough challenging for one night. Besides, she had other things on her mind.

'I think I'll go straight up to bed,' she said immediately they were inside the house.

'I'm having a nightcap first,' Blake returned. 'I'll join you shortly.'

Juliana did her best to keep her mind totally blank as she went through her night-time routine. She took off and hung up her clothes in the large Italian-designed walnut wardrobe; showered in her white-tiled gold-tapped bathroom; dried and powdered her body with a fragrant talc; cleaned her teeth; rubbed a light moisturiser into her face; took down and brushed out her hair.

This she stared at for a moment, thinking of Susanne's earlier comment about men not noticing changes their wives made to their appearance. It would be interesting, in a way, to see if Blake did notice. Hard not to. Several inches had been chopped off, leaving it to swing round her shoulders in a thick glossy curtain, the straight fringe lending mystery to her already exotic eyes.

Juliana never wore a nightie these days if she knew Blake was going to join her. It seemed coy to do so. Coyness was something she didn't like in women. If a wife was going to let her husband make love to her then why put clothes in the way? Maybe if he made love to her elsewhere in the house then it might be interesting to start with clothes on. But Blake had never done that.

What would she do if he ever did? How would she react?

Juliana's fingers tightened around her hairbrush as the most amazing fantasy started drifting into her mind. Agitated by it, she started vigorously brushing her hair, but soon her hand slowed to a stop and, while her eyes were wide open, it was not her reflection in the mirror that Juliana kept seeing, but another, heart-stopping vision...

Blake coming up behind her in the kitchen when she was cooking breakfast on a Saturday morning, wrapping his arms around her, pressing close so that she could feel his arousal through his bathrobe. She was also wearing a bathrobe under which she was similarly naked. He undid the sash, parting her robe to start playing with her breasts. Her breathing became very rapid, but she kept pretending to cook even though she was becoming uncontrollably excited inside. Only when his hands slid down between her thighs did she stop what she was doing. Whirling, she pulled his mouth down to hers in a savage kiss. Soon they sank down on to the kitchen floor, oblivious of the cold tiles, oblivious of everything but their passion for each other...

Suddenly, Juliana snapped back to reality, but the fantasy had left her with her heart pounding and her skin burning. She shook her head violently, trying to dispel more erotic thoughts from flooding her mind. Agitated by the effect they were having on her, she fled back into the bedroom, where she dived quickly in between the cool sheets.

Her mind, however, was relentless.

There followed the pool scenario... the dining-room... the sofa...

She squeezed her eyes tightly shut and huddled down under the quilt, but there was to be no peace in that either.

The shower... the stairs...

'Not asleep, are you?'

Her eyes flew open to encounter Blake closing the door, unsashing his robe as he walked towards the bed.

'No,' she gulped.

He smiled. God, but he was heart-stoppingly handsome when he smiled.

'And no headache?'

She shook her head.

He stared down at her. 'You've had your hair cut.'

Any satisfaction that he had noticed was over-shadowed by the tumultuous feelings racing through her at that moment. Half of her wanted him to part that robe, to let her see him in all his glorious nakedness. The other half was petrified at what she might do if this madness inside her got out of control.

'It suits you,' he said.

Her smile was jittery.

He stared down at her some more, his eyes travelling down her face and over her bare shoulders. The quilt was pulled up tightly over her breasts, which was just as well for Juliana knew full well that they were swollen, the nipples hard peaks of arousal.

'You looked lovely in your green velvet tonight, Juliana,' he said thickly, 'but you look even lovelier without anything on. I didn't realise till I saw you getting out of your bath last night what a truly perfect body you had. Don't hide it away from me, honey. Let me see you...'

Juliana panicked when he tried to extract the blanket from her suddenly clenched hands, her eyes widening into large frightened pools as she gazed up at him in panic-stricken alarm.

'I... I don't want you to.'

He stopped, a dark frown instantly marring his handsome features. 'Don't want me to do what? *Look* at you, or make love to you?'

'L-look at me.'

His sigh was definitely disgruntled. 'Why are you so damned shy?' he said, shrugging out of his robe and climbing in beside her. 'I'd understand if you were ugly perhaps, but by God, Juliana, you're gorgeous!'

Juliana said nothing, her heart pounding wildly as she felt his arousal brushing against her. Dear God, if he only knew! Her fantasies had just shown her her secret longings. She was simply dying to touch him, to show him the extent of her passion.

Shy? She could see now that her so-called shyness had been nothing but a blind, hiding her true self. Now, she wanted to snap that blind up, throw open the windows, let the light shine in. She wanted Blake to see her for the sensual woman she really was, to take that sensuality and explore it to the fullest.

But wanting and doing were two entirely different things. She had no real experience to fall back on. Besides, how could she suddenly start acting differently? Blake would think it strange. Still, he *had* just given her the opportunity to be a little bolder...

'I'm not *that* shy,' she said huskily, and trickled a tentative hand down his bare chest and over his stomach.

His muscles flinched beneath her fingers, his stomach tightening as he sucked in a startled breath.

'Don't...don't you want me to touch you?' she whispered shakily. Oh, how quickly could one's confidence be shattered! Juliana suddenly felt stupid and clumsy and totally inadequate.

Steely fingers tightened around hers. 'God, yes,' he groaned, and carried her hand to his eager flesh, showing her what he liked. 'Yes,' he urged. 'Just like that.'

When he left her to it, Juliana continued for several minutes, fascinated by the thrill of power she felt every time she made him groan or shudder. She was beginning to contemplate a more intimate foreplay when he suddenly loomed up to throw her back against the pillows, kissing her with such savagery that she thought she might suffocate. But it would have been a glorious suffocation!

'You don't know what you've started,' he growled at last, capturing her wrists and holding them wide on the bed. 'By God, woman, you should have let the devils lie. Now I won't be content with less than everything. Do you understand me?'

She merely stared up at him, eyes wide, heart thudding.

'*Do you understand me*?' he repeated, and shook her.

'Yes,' she rasped.

'Don't stop me this time,' he ground out, and, discarding her wrists, he threw back the blanket and began sliding down her exposed body, his mouth hot and merciless on her shivering, quivering flesh.

There was no question of stopping him. He was unstoppable anyway. But it soon became obvious to Juliana that there was so much she didn't know about sex, and so much that Blake did.

He sent her over the edge within seconds of reaching his goal. But instead of it being the end, it was only the beginning. Sometimes she felt like a rag-doll, pushed this way and that, a mindless receptacle for his almost insatiable passion. He wanted her every way he'd never had her before.

Even after he'd seemingly spilled every drop of seed into her, and they were collapsed together on the bed, Blake did not leave her alone, trailing his nails lightly over her swollen nipples, making sure he never let her come down from that plateau of sexual sensitivity and abandonment he seemed to have taken her to. Soon the desire to touch him back took possession of her. But her hands were not enough for him. He wanted her mouth as well. He *insisted*.

Dazedly, she complied, finding it a surprisingly arousing experience. And this was the way she achieved the unachievable, stirring him again till he could stand it no longer. It was then that he lifted her on to him, kneading her breasts quite roughly while he urged her to ride them both to another exhausting climax.

Hours passed. Dawn came. And they finally slept.

Yet when Juliana awoke, Blake was not in bed with her. She lay alone and naked on top of the sheets, a picture of decadent disarray. Her hair was tangled, her lips puffy, her thighs and breasts faintly bruised.

'Will an apology do? Or do you want a divorce?'

Juliana's legs shot up under her as she scrambled into a semi-sitting position, swivelling round on the bed in the direction of Blake's voice.

He was in the window-seat, his back against the frame, his knees up, still as stark naked as she was.

Juliana swallowed, reaching for a pillow to hug against herself. 'Why... why would I want either?'

His head turned slowly till their eyes met. Juliana was truly shocked. He looked almost haunted as though he'd just committed the most dreadful crime, when all he'd done was make love to his wife as he perhaps should have all along. OK, so he'd managed to put ten months' worth into one night. And he had been a touch brutal at times. But she'd never been in any real pain. At least, not any that she hadn't enjoyed.

There was a fine line, Juliana had discovered the previous night, between pleasure and pain. She licked dry lips at the thought of some of those razor-edged moments.

Blake was staring at her.

'Are you saying that you didn't mind the things I made you do last night?'

Juliana flushed fiercely, for she could not deny that daylight had a tendency to make some of their lovemaking seem incredibly uninhibited. But she wasn't ashamed of it. She loved Blake. She was his wife. Nothing they did together was wrong. If he was a little forceful then maybe she had needed him to be. She certainly hadn't wanted to go on enduring the sort of antiseptic, clinical sex they'd been having. Her love demanded more than that now. At least she might find some peace in carnal passion, if that was all Blake was capable of.

'No,' she said simply. 'I didn't mind. We're married, aren't we?'

'Might I remind you that married men have been charged with rape before today?' he returned drily.

'But you didn't rape me last night!'

'It felt as if I did.'

'Did it?' She was totally astounded at his un-doubted sincerity. 'But why?'

He glared at her. 'You ask me that? You, who shook with fear on our wedding night, who shud-dered whenever I tried to go past the most basic foreplay and intercourse, who even last night didn't want me to *look* at her. For God's sake, Juliana! What do you expect to think—that you suddenly went from prudish innocent to wanton whore in one night? Of course I forced you! If I didn't then ... then——' He broke off and looked at her as though he were seeing a ghost.

Oh, my God, she panicked. He's realised I've fallen in love with him.

Apparently not, however. For suddenly he swung his feet down from the window-seat and stood up, hands clenched by his side, uncaring if she saw that in his anger he had become sexually aroused. He glared at her across the room, and if looks could kill she would have shrivelled up on that bed right then and there.

Juliana cringed when he strode menacingly across the room, but he did not touch her, merely swept up his bathrobe from the floor and pulled it on, sashing it round his waist with angry movements. By the time he looked at her again, however, his face was a stony mask, all emotions carefully hidden away.

'If I thought for one moment,' he said in a tightly controlled voice, 'that it was my loyal assistant who'd corrupted you over this last three weeks then I would tear him limb from limb. Only my knowl-edge of Stewart Margin's ambition puts my mind at rest on that regard. He might fancy you—after all, what man wouldn't? But he would not dare put any secret desires of his into action. He knows what the penalty would be. The same goes for my business friends and acquaintances. That only leaves someone you work with. Your resignation goes in first thing Monday morning, Juliana. If not, I'll start divorce proceedings immediately.'

CHAPTER SEVEN

JULIANA gaped up at him while the import of his words sank in.

'I take it by your silence that you will do as I say,' he drawled. 'After all, I'm sure you want to continue as Mrs Blake Preston, don't you, Juliana?'

Did she?

'In that case we won't mention the matter of your little indiscretion again,' he finished coldly, and, turning, strode from the room, leaving the door open behind him.

Juliana stared at the empty doorway for a few seconds before throwing the pillow away and dashing after Blake.

His bedroom was empty. Where had he gone? The sound of the shower running sent her hurtling into his bathroom, uncaring of his privacy, uncaring of her own nudity, uncaring of anything but the need to give voice to the fury welling up within her. She banged back the sliding glass door to reveal a naked Blake standing there under a steaming jet of hot water, his face upturned, his eyes shut. He didn't flinch an inch, or open his eyes, or turn her way.

'How dare you?' she spat. 'How *dare* you? I have not even *looked* at another man during our marriage, let alone slept with one. For you to imply...no, not imply, *accuse* me of being un-

faithful while you were away, of doing with some
other man the sort of things we did last night, why
I . . . I . . . words fail me!'

She scooped in some much needed air. Her whole
body was shaking uncontrollably. But even in her
rage some inner instinct warned her to be careful
with what she said, what she admitted. 'Has it ever
occurred to you I might have become a little bored
with our sex-life?' she ranted on. 'For it had become
boring, Blake. Even you must recognise that.
Boring and predictable. And maybe I've become
dissatisfied with the way you never touch me unless
it's in bed. A wife likes her husband to show
outward signs of affection occasionally.'

Now Blake opened his eyes to look at her. They
were hard and disbelieving. Juliana put her hands
on her hips in a gesture of defiance and outrage.
'I have *not* taken a lover, either at work or any
other place. And I will *not* resign on Monday! If
that means you are going to divorce me, then so be
it! Nothing, not being your wife or all the money
in the world, is worth having to give up my independence and self-respect! To tell the truth, I
can't imagine why I agreed to marry you in the first
place, Blake Preston. You'd have to be the most
selfish, cold-blooded, monstrous man in the entire
world!'

The hands that shot out to grab her came so fast
that she'd been yanked into the shower before she
could say Jack Robinson. Blake slammed her hard
against the wet tiles, holding her hands captive
on either side of her, jamming one solid thigh
between hers.

'Is that so?' he ground out, his sneering mouth only inches from hers. 'Well, in that case you won't be surprised to hear I don't believe a word you've just said. But you've got guts, Juliana, I'll give you that. *And* imagination. Bored, were you? Dissatisfied, were you? Then why didn't you say something? You're an intelligent woman. You must have known any man would have wanted more than what you were giving me.'

His water-slicked knee lifted to start rubbing between her legs, making her breath catch and her stomach tighten. She knew she shouldn't respond beneath such an outrageous caress, but she did. Dear God, she did! His mouth curved into a cynical smile.

'You've suddenly discovered sex, Juliana,' he mocked. 'And you didn't discover it with me. That's the truth of it, my treacherous little wife. But I've always been a man to try to turn disadvantage to advantage. If it's imaginative sex you want, then I'm sure I can keep this new appetite of yours well satisfied.'

She gasped as he moved his other leg between hers, holding her there against the wall while he manoeuvred his impassioned flesh into her shockingly ready body. She turned her face away in appalled horror at the pleasure she felt, the mad excitement that took possession of her as he set up a relentlessly erotic rhythm. The water cascaded down over his head, splashing into her parted lips, trickling down over her distended nipples.

'Is this what you want?' he said, his voice slurred.

She wanted to scream her denial but no words came from her panting mouth. And then she was shuddering against the wall, her knees going from under her. He lifted her then, carrying her limp, wet body back into his bedroom, spreading her out across his bed where he continued quite mercilessly till he too spasmed with a violent release.

Almost immediately, he levered himself up from her shattered body, staring down into her utterly drained face with eyes like hell.

'Keep your job,' he grated. 'But God help you if I ever catch you with another man again.'

He turned and went back into the still running shower, this time locking the door behind him.

If she'd been in her own room, Juliana would have curled up where she was and cried her eyes out. But the possibility that Mrs Dawson might come upstairs at any moment to do the bedrooms sent her stumbling back to her own room and her own bathroom. She too locked the door, leaning against it and letting the tears run unashamedly down her face.

She spent ages in the bathroom, bathing at length. And thinking long and hard.

The marriage was doomed, she finally decided. Doomed...

Yet to simply throw in the towel when she loved the man so much seemed a cowardly thing to do. More than cowardly—extremely difficult, considering the changed nature of their sexual relationship.

Who would have believed she could be so easily and devastatingly satisfied as Blake had satisfied her in that shower? How did you turn your back on such pleasure?

But she had to if she was going to live with herself. Life was more than the physical. And so was a marriage.

When she finally came out of the bathroom, the bed had been made with fresh sheets, the room tidied and dusted. Juliana blushed to think of what Susanne might have thought about the state of the bed. She pulled on jeans and a top, and was standing there, trying to decide what to do next, when there was a knock on the door.

'Juliana... It's Blake...'

'C-come in,' she stammered, instantly nervous. Now was the moment to tell him she could not go on if he really believed she was an unfaithful wife; if he was going to continue to treat her with contempt.

Surprised to find him dressed as though for work in a business suit, Juliana was at a loss for words for a moment. Blake, however, was not similarly indisposed.

'I've decided to fly to Sydney this afternoon,' he began straight away, standing with his hand still on the doorknob. 'I'll be back on Wednesday evening in time to take you to the races on Thursday. Before you say anything, I want to apologise, not for my behaviour—since you undoubtedly enjoyed what I did,' he inserted drily, 'but for my accusations of adultery, and my rather lack-lustre performance during this marriage so far. I mistakenly thought the type of sex-life we had was all you could handle. Obviously I didn't see the signs of change. Maybe

I've also left you alone too much, a factor which will be remedied.'

He sighed then. It was a weary, troubled sigh. 'I don't want to lose you, Juliana. I value our marriage and I want it to last. Maybe it's time we started trying for a child.'

A *child*? A child would bind her to him forever. There would be no escape. Juliana needed that escape for a while. Much as Blake's words just now had soothed most of her doubts and fears, she still wasn't entirely convinced their marriage would last.

'I . . . I think we should wait a while for that, Blake,' she returned hesitantly. 'At least till the New Year, the way we planned.'

His gaze locked on to hers, his eyes intent. What was he trying to see?

'Very well, Juliana,' he conceded matter-of-factly. 'Goodbye. I'll see you on Wednesday. You can tell Mrs Dawson I should be home for dinner.'

And then he was gone.

Juliana sighed. What had changed? No goodbye kiss. No asking her to accompany him to the airport. No doubt she would not hear from him during the days he was gone, since three days would hardly warrant a phone call in Blake's opinion.

Juliana was wrong about that. He did call. Every night. At first, she was thrilled, but then not. The calls were brief and rather brusque. Clearly he was checking up her, seeing if she came home every evening. When he called her again at work on Wednesday morning she was quite sharp with him, even though he was only telling her that he would be taking her out for dinner that night and that she was to inform Mrs Dawson not to cook for them. After she'd hung up, she regretted her sharpness, but she couldn't help suspecting that Blake had been trying to catch her out at something at work.

As luck would have it, she was kept late at work that day. Blake was already home when she turned into the driveway for there was a light on in his bedroom. As Juliana used the remote control to open the garage doors, a nervous agitation churned her stomach.

She knew why.

Not a night had gone by since Blake left that she hadn't wanted him. Quite fiercely. Yet, with the passing of the days, that mad night she'd spent with him, plus the incident in the shower, had taken on an unreal feeling. It was as though it hadn't happened to her and Blake, but to two other people. Strangers. Juliana worried that Blake would never be like that again, that *she* would never feel like that again.

The kitchen was deserted as Juliana walked through from the garage. She had given Susanne the night off in view of her not having to cook for them, and the housekeeper was happy enough to visit her sister who lived in the Dandenong Hills. She wouldn't be back till the next day.

There was only herself and Blake in the huge house. The thought excited Juliana. She hoped it would excite him.

He didn't look at all excited, standing at his dressing-table, putting his gold cuff-links into the sleeves of an ivory silk shirt. The front buttons were undone and the shirt hung open, showing an expanse of smooth golden flesh down to where his charcoal-grey trousers stopped the unconsciously sensual display. He glanced up once he became aware of her standing in the doorway, watching him. It was a very fleeting glance.

'Ah, there you are, Juliana.' Not a word of enquiry or reproach about her being late. 'I've booked a table for seven-thirty. You've only got thirty minutes. Look, why don't you leave your hair up, have a quick shower and put on that green velvet dress you had on the other night? I really liked that on you and it won't need ironing.''

He finished with his cuff-links and started buttoning up his shirt. When she continued to stand there, staring at him, he lifted an eyebrow at her. 'Is there something I can do for you?' he drawled.

She tried not to flush at the image in her mind.

'No. I was going to ask how things went in Sydney but it can wait, I suppose.' And, whirling away, she fled to her room, closing her eyes in pained humiliation as she shut the door behind her.

Twenty-five minutes later she was struggling to pull up the back zip of the emerald-green velvet when Blake materialised behind her. 'Let me . . .'

Her eyes flew to his in the dressing-table mirror, but he merely smiled that enigmatic smile he sometimes produced and zipped her up. Yet his hands lingered on her shoulders, his gaze admiring as it travelled slowly over the reflected dress in the mirror. Juliana found herself looking at the dress as well, trying to control the wild fluttering of her heart.

It was a simple style, cut to hug the line of a woman's body, the skirt pencil-slim and just above the knee. The sleeves were three-quarter-length and tight, emphasising the slenderness of her arms. But it was the neckline that drew the eyes, the wide sweetheart shape showing a good deal of creamy flesh and just a hint of cleavage.

Juliana had first discovered the style suited her figure when she'd worn Barbara's graduation gown, and since then she had often bought dresses with that neckline. The only drawback was that bra straps often showed, so the right underwear was required.

Juliana always wore a strapless corselette of stretch black lace with this particular dress, since such a garment also enhanced the hour-glass shape that best displayed the tightly fitted style. Her years of modelling had taught her how to show her figure off to best advantage. Such underwear pulled in her waist, giving her slender hips a fuller look, and pushing up her limited bust.

Thinking about her underwear, however, especially with Blake standing so close behind her, was making Juliana hotly aware of her body.

'I have a little present for you,' he astonished her by saying.

She went to turn around but he held her there with an iron grip. 'No, stay right where you are...'

Drawing a long green velvet case from his suit jacket pocket, he unclipped it and placed it on the dressing-table in front of her. In it was the most beautiful emerald and gold necklace Juliana had ever seen.

'Oh, Blake! It's magnificent!' she exclaimed, reaching out to run her fingers over it. Clearly, he had had the green dress in mind when he'd bought it. 'But . . . but what's it for?' She glanced up at his face in the mirror. 'It's not my birthday for another month.'

His smile was odd as he lifted the necklace from its velvet bed and secured it around her neck. There was no doubt that it looked spectacular against her pale flesh but Juliana had the strangest feeling that with this gift Blake had just paid for services rendered. Or was it for services still to *be* rendered?

'Does it have to be for anything?' he said suavely. 'Can't I give my beautiful wife a gift?'

'Yes, but . . .'

She froze when he bent to kiss her neck. 'Do shut up, Juliana, and just let me do things to please you. Isn't that what you said you wanted? Outward displays of affection? From now on I will give you whatever takes my fancy. And *do* whatever takes my fancy . . .'

His mouth trailed lightly back up to her right ear, where he blew softly into the shell-like cavern. Juliana shivered.

'Perhaps we'd better be going,' he said softly.

Dinner at the restaurant was agony.

First, Blake had booked one of those ghastly places where people went not so much to eat, but to be seen. Celebrities and millionaires abounded. Most of the men had little dolly-birds on their arms: not wives—mistresses and girlfriends. And they all dripped with expensive jewellery.

Juliana's new emerald necklace felt as if it was lit in neon around her neck, especially after one abominable woman made caustic mention of it. *Kept woman*, Juliana felt it was screaming out to everyone. Which was crazy really. Blake was her husband. How could that make her *kept* in any way?

Yet by the time they left the restaurant Juliana was very much on edge.

'I didn't like that place, Blake,' she said with a little shudder. 'I don't want to go there ever again.'

'Oh? What was wrong with it?'

'The food stinks and so does the clientele.'

He laughed. 'You don't like the rich and famous any more?'

'I never did like them, as you very well know. I merely envied the power they had.'

'So if you couldn't beat them, you joined them, is that it? After all, might I remind you that your husband is a very rich man?'

'No, you don't have to remind me...' Her hand lifted to finger the necklace.

He slanted her a dark look but said nothing. Silence was maintained till they were climbing out of the car inside the garages.

'The night's still young,' Blake said. 'Care for a swim?'

'I...I don't think so.' The pool had become the focus of Juliana's most persistent fantasy lately.

'What, then? You tell me what you want to do.'

His eyes clashed with hers over the roof of the car. Why did she get the feeling he was taunting her, trying to make her say that she wanted him to make love to her? Was this to be her punishment for changing the status quo in their relationship? Constant humiliation?

Juliana fiercely resented being put in such a position. No way was she going to beg, or grovel, or even hint.

'I don't know about you,' she said casually, 'but I have a good book to read.'

'Oh? Anything I've read?'

To be caught out in a lie made Juliana's teeth clamp down hard in her jaw. 'I doubt it,' she bit out, vowing to snatch up anything from the family room on the way through. Susanne was always reading.

'You don't want a nightcap?'

'Well ... maybe a port before I go up.' To race away would seem as if she was frightened to be alone with him.

'You didn't ask me what happened in Sydney,' he remarked while he poured them both a port.

Juliana was settled in one of the three gold brocade armchairs that matched the sofa. The sofa, like the pool, had been put on her list of no-nos for a while. She took the glass with a stiff smile on her lips. 'Sorry, but I'm sure you handled things with your usual panache.'

'*Panache*? What kind of business term is that? Panache, I ask you!' He dropped down in one of the other armchairs, stretching his legs out in front of him and loosening his tie. 'I gave those lazy, inefficient idiots up there a blast that could have been heard all the way to Melbourne. I doubt they'd be telling their wives tonight that their boss has *panache*.'

'Sounds as if you were in a bad mood,' she pointed out.

'Maybe.' He shot her a knowing look. 'Maybe I had good cause...'

'Meaning?'

'Meaning I would have much rather been here, making mad, passionate love to my wife.'

Juliana's hand shook as she lifted the port to her suddenly dry lips. She sipped the drink, her gaze finding Blake's over the rim. There was self-mockery in those glittering blue eyes, but real desire as well. Her stomach lurched.

'Take off your clothes,' he said abruptly.

Some of the port spilt into her lap. 'Oh, my God, my beautiful dress!' She shot Blake a savage glance. 'You made me do that,' she accused. 'You, with your pathetic suggestions.'

He laughed and stood up. 'It's you who's pathetic, Juliana.' He came over and dabbed at the spilt port with the scarlet hankie he had in his pocket. Leaning over, he kissed her full on the mouth then fixed ruthless eyes upon her. 'You've been on fire for sex all night and what have you done? Complained. Quibbled. *Lied*. Why not come right out and say you want me to ravage you? Why not stand up and take that damned dress right off? It's what you want to do, isn't it? Or would you really prefer to go to bed with a good book?'

He lanced her stunned face with a furious glare before straightening to stride back over to the bar. 'To hell with this port. I need a real drink!'

He rattled the whisky decanter, even spilling some as he filled a fresh and very tall glass. 'Here's to a return to prudery!' he announced, and lifted the glass in a mocking toast. But when he turned around to further deride the woman who had ignited such an uncharacteristic display of temper and emotion, Blake froze.

She stood before him, the dress on the floor, her body the epitome of erotica in the black lace corselette, her long slender legs encased in sheer black stockings that ran all the way down to her black high heels. The emerald necklace around her neck looked exotic and somewhat depraved. Her breathing, he noted, was rapid, and there was a wild light blazing in her eyes. She had never looked more dangerously seductive or more breathtaking beautiful.

'You bitch,' he rasped, and, putting the glass down, moved slowly towards her, a smile on his lips.

CHAPTER EIGHT

JULIANA'S chin lifted. 'If I'm a bitch, then what are you?' she countered, well aware that she was being deliberately provocative. But, having taken up Blake's challenge, no way was she going to back down.

'Oh, I'm a bastard through and through,' her husband agreed, his smile turning rueful as he reached out to touch the emerald necklace around her throat. 'But a very rich bastard, you must admit,' he added, and, curling his fingers around the necklace, he began pulling her towards him.

The taunt over his wealth added a fiery fury to Juliana's already heated bloodstream. When her head was yanked indignantly backwards, the clasp gave way and Blake was left holding the broken necklace in his hand.

'Don't you ever throw your money in my face again!' she hissed. 'And don't you ever parade me in front of other people like some cheap whore!' Snatching the necklace from his stunned fingers, she flung it across the room. 'That's what I think of your thinking you can buy me!'

Too late Juliana realised she had finally done what she'd always thought she wanted to do to her unrufflable husband: make him really lose his temper. But the actuality was not quite as desirable as she had once imagined. Blake looked as if he wanted to kill her.

'I don't have to buy you,' he ground out savagely. 'You're my wife! I can damned well have you any time I want you.' And, with his face flushing an angry red, he scooped her up into his arms and dumped her on to the sofa, pinning her there with a knee across her stomach while he began reefing his clothes off: first his tie, then his jacket and shirt till he was naked to the waist.

Only then did he turn his attention to *her* attire, reefing open the hooks that ran down the front of the black lace corselette and wrenching both flaps aside, exposing her body to his glittering gaze. Holding her shoulders down, he sat on the edge of the sofa, effectively stopping her from escaping. When his mouth started to descend towards one of her hard-tipped breasts Juliana lashed out with closed fists, striking the side of his head, his shoulders, his chest.

'No you can't damned well have me any time you want me!' she screamed at him. 'Not unless I agree.'

His smile was frightening as he gripped her flailing hands in an iron grasp. 'You'll agree all right, my sexy Juliana. You'll agree...' And, pinioning both her wrists within one large male hand, his free hand set out to make his prophecy come true, sliding down over her flat stomach and under the elastic of her tiny black lace bikini briefs.

'No,' she groaned once he found his target.

'Yes,' he bit out, and ruthlessly continued.

'You're a bastard.'

'We've already established that.'

'I . . . I won't give in,' she cried, but her voice was already unsteady, her heart hammering away like mad.

Gritting her teeth, she tried to ignore the sensations his knowing hand was evoking, tried not to let her thighs fall evocatively apart to give him easier access to her body. But she was fighting a losing battle. In the end, pride demanded she not let him win, even as she lost.

Catching his heavy-lidded gaze with a desire-charged look of her own, she smiled a smile as perversely wicked as his had been. His eyes widened, that tormenting hand stilling for a moment.

'Don't stop,' she husked, and arched her back in voluptuous surrender.

His hand withdrew as he stood up, his breathing as ragged as her own. 'No,' he said thickly. 'You won't get what you want that easily. You'll earn your pleasure, wife.'

'What makes you think I won't enjoy earning it?' she rasped, and levered herself up into a sitting position, her hands going to the belt on his trousers.

His fingers closed over hers, then tightened. Her eyes flew upwards, locking with his. The pain of the buckle digging into her palm was intense but she refused to make a sound. Finally, he laughed and drew her upwards till she was standing, trembling, before him. A few violent movements and he had stripped her totally naked, except for the long black stockings and her high heels.

For an interminable time he simply stared at her, his torrid gaze roving over her softly parted lips, her swollen breasts, the triangle of damp curls that so ineffectually guarded her desire. When he reached out to touch her there, she sucked in a shuddering breath.

'Juliana,' he said, and with a groan of raw need moved to crush her against him, grabbing the back of her head and covering her mouth with his till she was weak and pliant in his arms.

'And now, my incredibly beautiful wife,' he muttered at last against her panting mouth, 'let's see just how far you'll let your bastard of a husband go...'

'Wake up, sleepyhead.'

Juliana yawned and stretched, then buried her face back in the pillow. 'Can't,' she mumbled. 'Too tired.'

'I don't doubt it,' Blake muttered drily. 'But we have to get going. If we're not at Flemington by eleven we won't get a parking spot, even in the members' area. It's nine already.'

'Nine!' Juliana shot upright, pushing her hair out of her face. 'My God!' she exclaimed, looking around her. 'I'm in *your* room. When did we...?' Her frown was puzzled, for the last thing she recalled was falling asleep in Blake's arms on the sofa.

'I carried you up,' he told her on a sardonic note. 'And believe me, I won't do it again in a hurry. Either you weigh a ton or I was a little—er—done in at the time.'

Laughter bubbled from her lips. Some time during their crazed lovemaking session last night all the anger and frustration associated with their changing sexual relationship had been routed.

They'd mocked each other, taunted each other, dared each other. They'd even hurt each other. Juliana could remember slapping Blake once, and he'd slapped her right back.

But the final outcome had been a purging that left them both exhausted, yet at peace with each other. Afterwards, Blake had cradled Juliana in his arms and told her that there would never be another woman for him. Never.

It might not have been an avowal of love, but it was as close as he would ever come to it. Juliana had drifted off into a deep sleep, happy and content.

She had woken just as happy. 'You should know better than to challenge your old diving mate, shouldn't you?' she teased.

Blake smiled from where he was lying next to her, his arms linked behind his head. 'They were great days, weren't they, Julianna?'

'Marvellous...'

'Too bad we had to grow up and become part of the world at large. It's not a very nice place.'

Juliana's heart turned over at Blake's sudden bleakness of spirit. She much preferred the man he'd been last night, the lover who'd cuddled her close and said the sweetest of things.

'No, it's not,' she agreed, 'but we can make our own little corner a nice place, can't we?'

His head turned towards her, and a small smile tugged the grimness from his mouth. 'My darling Juliana... the eternal optimist.'

'I'll settle for being just your darling Juliana,' she whispered, and kissed him on the cheek. 'I do so love being your wife, Blake. I love everything about it. Now more than ever.'

She saw his hesitation to accept her love, despite her having skirted around saying straight out that she loved him. In the end, he couldn't help withdrawing from any open acceptance, defusing a situation he obviously found awkward with a flash of dry humour.

'I know exactly what *you* love, Mrs Preston, and I'm not going to be conned into any more. As it is, I'm going to have to take a bottle of vitamin E tablets with breakfast, plus a swag of oysters for lunch. Speaking of lunch, up you get, lazy-bones. The gee-gees await!'

He himself bounced out of bed and headed straight for the shower without looking back. Juliana noted that he carefully locked the door behind him.

She shrugged away any upsurge of dismay. Blake was not about to change in a hurry. But he *was* changing. After all, he hadn't put her in her own bed when he'd carried her up, had he? He'd put her in *his*.

'This place is madness today!' Juliana exclaimed, looking at the cars pouring into Flemington. And it was only ten-forty!

Blake had managed to squeeze his turquoise Mercedes sports car into a smallish spot near a fence, not far from the members' entrance into the track. As was the tradition during the Melbourne Cup carnival, people had set up picnics behind and between their cars, with caviare and chicken and champagne on the menu, but still more people were surging towards the gates of the course proper, anxious to soak up the atmosphere inside the grounds.

'It was worse on Tuesday, I heard,' Blake said, coming round to join her at the back of the car. 'Something like a hundred buses parked down along the Maribyrnong River, and countless limousines dropping off Arab sheikhs and their entourages all morning.'

'How would you know?' she frowned. 'You were in Sydney.'

He grinned. 'Stayed in the motel and watched it on telly. Can't miss the Melbourne Cup, you know. I'm a Melbournian!'

'I suppose you even backed the winner.'

'Of course. I had half the field.'

'Blake! You can't win punting like that.'

'Juliana, my sweet . . .'

She caught her breath when he put a protective arm around her to steer her safely through the milling crowd.

'. . . one doesn't try to win on the Melbourne Cup. One tries to end up with a ticket on the winner. That's totally different. After the race, one surreptitiously slips all the dead tickets into nearby waste-paper baskets then produces the winning one. Everyone thinks you're a genius!'

Juliana laughed and shook her head. 'I won't from now on. I'll know the truth.'

'Ah, yes, but . . .' he gave her an affectionate squeeze—in public! '. . . I don't mind *you* knowing the truth. There shouldn't be any secrets between a husband and wife, should there?'

Juliana's heart turned over. Tears hovered, but she quickly blinked them back and lifted a dazzling smile to his handsome face. 'No, Blake. No secrets. None at all.'

He stared down at her for a second, and she could have sworn a dark cloud flitted momentarily across his eyes. It worried her. Did he still think she might have had an affair? Oh, surely not.

'Blake...'

'Mmm?'

'I...' She glanced around her. People were pressing close. The words died in her throat. Which was just as well, perhaps. The more she protested her innocence, the more guilty she might sound. Best say nothing.

'Oh, nothing,' she went on with an offhand wave of her hand. 'It's going to be warm, isn't it? I'm glad I wore something reasonably cool.'

The pink linen suit she had on was very simple, with short sleeves, a straight skirt and big black buttons down the front of the jacket. Teamed with a saucy black hat that dipped over one side of her face, and other black patent accessories, Juliana thought she looked chic and cool.

'It'll probably storm later,' Blake remarked, glancing up at the sky. 'I hope that hat doesn't ruin.'

'The lady in the hat shop warned me it would go like a limp rag if I ever got it wet. Do you honestly think it will rain?'

'Sure to by the end of the day.'

'We can stay under cover, sipping champagne.'

'I came here to have a bet, Juliana, not sip champagne.'

'I thought you came here today to be with me! Truly, Blake, everyone from work is dying to meet you. Now you tell me you're going to be slipping away to spend all afternoon fighting your way through to the bookmakers or standing in long totalisator queues. You do realise the promotional marquees are in the middle of the course proper, don't you?'

'Good God, why didn't they get one of the decent ones down the end of the straight?'

'Don't be such a snob. There's nothing wrong with our being in the centre. Firstly, you'll get a much better view of the races. Special tiered seats are being set up near the finishing-post. You couldn't be in a better spot. And the company has hired a couple of hostesses whose job it is to go round putting everyone's bets on for them. What more could you ask for?'

'You ... and me ... naked ... on a desert island?'

Heat zoomed into her cheeks. 'Don't say such things out loud,' she hissed, aware of the people all around her.

Blake's chuckle was cynical as he leant close. 'You can't fool me any more with that prim and proper act. I know the real you, Juliana. I only hope none of the other gentlemen here today knows the real you as well...'

Her eyes jerked up to his. 'You ... you still don't trust me, do you?'

'I put trust in the same category as love, my sweet. It's very nice in theory but awfully suspect in practice.'

Any further chit-chat was terminated by their arrival at the toll gates. Blake withdrew his wallet and paid the entrance fees, after which he took her elbow and urged her inside.

'Don't get your knickers in a knot, Juliana,' he pronounced brusquely on seeing her distress. 'I don't believe in worrying about things one can't change, which includes the past. We've started our marriage anew this past week with a clean slate and a damned sight more interesting sex-life. Let's leave it at that, shall we?

'Of course,' he added darkly as they walked together past the beds of roses and down towards where they could cross into the centre of the track, 'I would cast a dim view if any man here today showed any more than a work-like interest in you. A very dim view indeed . . .'

No man dared.

Blake, in full millionaire mode, was a formidable husband and companion. It would have taken a brave male to try to muscle in on the woman on *his* arm, especially when that woman was his wife! Juliana still gained the impression that Blake sized up every one of her colleagues, from the nineteen-year-old mailboy to the thirty-three-year-old field sales manager to the national sales manager, who was pushing fifty and very happily married.

Juliana had to work hard to hide her frustration with Blake. What did she have to do to persuade him that she hadn't been playing around while he was away?

Nothing, she finally realised. He would believe what he wanted to believe. To change her behaviour for fear of feeding his ill-founded suspicions was not only non-productive but extremely stressful. She felt tense enough as it was, having Blake give everyone the once-over with that penetrating gaze of his.

The women, she noticed, stared at him openly and swooned behind his back. And why not? He was like a young Robert Redford with his classically featured face, blond hair and blue eyes, not to mention his tall, athletic body, encased very attractively that day in an elegantly casual tan suit and open-necked blue shirt. All this, plus the fact that he was as wealthy as any Onassis, made her handsome husband pack a pretty powerful punch.

'I think it's the wrong spouse doing the worrying,' she muttered under her breath on one occasion.

Blake shot her a dry look over his shoulder then returned to give his bet to the simpering hostess.

They all traipsed out to see the race in question—the third of the day. Juliana's choice stumbled out of the barrier and was never sighted. Blake's was beaten by a short half-head.

'If I'd been putting on my own bets,' he grumbled, 'I'd have had the winner.'

'Sure,' she said ruefully. 'You'd also have had every other horse in the race, even the donkey I bet on.'

'True,' he grinned.

They were still sitting on the seats near the winning-post, everyone else having gone back inside their respective marquees.

Juliana glanced up at the sky. Black clouds were sweeping in from the west, a sure sign of the storm Blake had predicted earlier.

She sighed. 'I suppose we'd better get back under cover. It's looking mighty ominous overhead. Good grief!' she suddenly exclaimed. 'Do you see who I see over there?'

She nodded over to where Owen Hawthorne was standing near the rails on the other side of the track, arm in arm with none other than Virginia Blakenthorp. It was the first time Juliana had seen either of them since her marriage, which was not surprising, she supposed, since Blake didn't socialise with his old crowd any more.

'If you mean our respective exes,' he said in a bored tone, 'then yes . . . I see them.'

'Do you think they might be going out with each other now?'

'I certainly should hope so. They're engaged.'

Juliana sucked in a startled breath. 'Owen's *engaged* to Virginia?'

Blake settled narrowed eyes upon her. 'Yes. Why? Does that bother you?'

'Well, I . . . I . . . no, not really. I'm sure they're admirably suited. But if you knew that, why didn't you tell me?'

He shrugged. 'I didn't think you'd be interested.'

'I'm not *interested*. I'm just . . . just . . .'

'Jealous?' Blake suggested blandly.

Juliana glared her exasperation. 'It's not a matter of jealousy, but of guilt.'

'*Guilt*?'

'Yes, guilt. I felt guilty getting married so quickly after I broke my engagement to Owen. He loved me, you know, despite his shortcomings. I wasn't totally insensitive to his feelings. Virginia I wasn't so concerned with. Girls like her rarely stir me to sympathy. But I didn't like either of them to think I only married you for your money.'

'But you *did* marry me for my money, darling. I knew that from the start. It was my ace card in securing your services as a wife. Of course, it has taken some time for my investment to bear fruit...'

He leant over and kissed her with almost insulting tenderness. Juliana gasped when his lips finally lifted from hers, her eyes pained as she looked up at him. But her pain soon changed to a justifiable anger.

'There are many wealthy men in this world,' she snapped, 'whom I wouldn't touch with a bargepole, let alone marry. If it were just your money I wanted, Blake, then why do I still work, why do I always insist on buying my own clothes and paying my way?'

His shrug was indifferent. 'Very well, so I used the wrong word. You married me for my position and power. Why deny it? I've never minded, Juliana. You know that. I've always admired your honest ambition. I especially admired your refusal to pretend love, quite unlike that lying bitch over there.'

The venom in Blake's voice gave rise to the unnerving suspicion that he might really have been in love with Virginia. Maybe he still was. His assertion that night that he'd broken his engagement because Virginia wanted to become a lady of leisure after their marriage suddenly didn't ring true.

'What really happened with Virginia, Blake? Did you find out she had another lover?'

'No,' he returned coldly. 'I found out her family was stony-broke, yet the day before she'd been telling me what a killing her daddy had made on the Stock Exchange that year. I suddenly realised she wouldn't look at me twice without my money. Hell, during those months of near-bankruptcy most of my so-called friends deserted me in droves. I thought Virginia was different from the usual society girl because she worked. But she was only working because she *needed* to work, not because she wanted to. I was nothing to her but a meal-ticket, a means for her to embrace the type of empty, lunch-flitting, charity-committee existence females of her ilk thrive on!'

He lanced Juliana with a savage scowl. 'Now, if you're finished with the third degree about *my* life, why don't I hear some truths about yours? Have you been seeing Owen Hawthorne while I've been away?'

'No!'

'Who, then?'

'No one!'

'Don't lie to me, Juliana.'

'I am *not* lying to you.'

'You'd better not be. I thought I could let by-gones be bygones but I've suddenly realised I'm not that noble. There are some things in life that a man just cannot tolerate being deceived about, and his wife's extra-curricular activities is one of them. If I ever find out you *have* lied to me in this, Juliana, you might discover a Blake you've never seen before.'

He stood up abruptly. 'Come on, let's go back inside before this storm breaks right over our heads.'

Stunned by Blake's clearly jealous warning, Juliana said very little for the rest of the afternoon. Was his jealousy inspired by male ego and possessiveness? she kept wondering. Or something far deeper and more vulnerable?

She dared not hope Blake was falling in love with her, but somehow she couldn't help hoping. It was what she wanted more than anything else in the world. Why, if Blake loved her, she could endure anything. Anything at all!

Not, however, his sister Barbara, who was waiting for them when they arrived home that afternoon.

CHAPTER NINE

THERE was no warning of Barbara's presence inside as Blake parked his car and cut the engine. No strange car taking up one of the two empty spaces in the four car garage, or parked in the street outside. The first they knew of their unexpected visitor was when they came into the kitchen.

'There's someone to see you, Mr Preston,' Susanne announced in her starchy Mrs Dawson voice. 'Your sister. She's in the study.'

Juliana grimaced, turning away to place her hat and bag on the breakfast bar. Susanne saw the reaction and almost smiled, but managed to hold herself together. Clearly, she didn't like Barbara any more than Juliana did.

'She seemed upset,' the housekeeper added.

Blake frowned. 'I see... Maybe I'll go in and talk to her alone, Juliana,' he said, glancing at her over his shoulder.

'Be my guest,' she returned drily.

He shot her an exasperated look. 'Women!' he grumped. And marched off.

'What's up, do you know?' Juliana asked as soon as Blake was out of earshot.

Susanne shrugged. 'Mr Preston's sister wouldn't confide in me. Maybe she's left her husband. Or maybe he's thrown her out.' She turned away and continued her preparations for the evening meal.

136

'I presume I should cook enough for one more for tonight's dinner?'

Juliana groaned silently. Having Barbara over for the odd meal was bad enough. But to have her stay didn't bear thinking about.

'I suppose so,' she sighed. 'I sure hope that's all you'll have to do for her.'

The housekeeper's eyes jerked up. 'I hope so too! If there's one woman I can't stand it's...' Suddenly she bit her bottom lip and busied herself back on the vegetables. 'Sorry, Juliana. I shouldn't have said that. It's none of my business. Mr Preston can have here whomever he likes. My job is just to do the housework, not voice opinions.'

Juliana patted the other woman on the shoulder. 'It's all right, Susanne, I understand your feelings entirely. The woman's a right pain in the butt. But, as you say, she is Blake's sister and we must make her as welcome as we can. Of course, if you decide to short-sheet the bed and add the odd funnelweb spider to her night-time glass of water then I'll turn a blind eye.'

Both women burst into laughter, and were still giggling when Blake strode back into the room, looking like thunder.

'Might I request a pot of black coffee?' he said sharply. 'That crazy female in there has been downing my Johnny Walker like water, along with some damned tranquilliser or something. I can't get any sense out of her. Bring the coffee in when it's ready, would you, Juliana? Maybe you, being a woman, might be able to get to the bottom of the problem. All Barbara's done since I walked in is cry! And before you tell me you and she don't get along—as if I didn't know that already—then just do it for me, OK?'

'Of course, Blake,' Juliana agreed. 'I'll do what I can.'

'Thank you.' And, whirling, he was gone as abruptly as he'd come.

Susanne shook her head then started making the coffee. 'Men aren't too good at just listening, are they?'

Juliana frowned. 'Blake used to be when he was younger...'

'Was he? Oh, well, I didn't know him them.'

'He was very nice. Very kind and considerate.'

'*Was* he?' There was no doubting the surprise in the housekeeper's voice.

Juliana's smile was rather sad. 'He's still like that underneath,' she said. 'It's just that life's been hard on him, what with his mother's suicide, his father's premature death and then his having to work so hard to save the family company from bankruptcy. He had to become tough to survive, I guess. When men have to be like that at work all day, they don't always know how to switch off when they come home.'

'You're probably right. My Fred was a bus driver. He used to tell me that by the time he came home after driving in the traffic all day his nerves were shot to pieces.'

'That's probably why he played golf,' Juliana suggested. 'It's supposed to be a very relaxing game. Your husband would have especially appreciated all that walking in wide open spaces.'

'Yes...' Susanne seemed thoughtful while she put he finishing touches on the coffee-tray. 'Yes, I uppose that could have been so.' She brightened ls she handed Juliana the tray. 'I always thought le just wanted to get away from me. But I can see low that he might have *needed* that relaxation. As t was, he still had a heart attack before he should ave...'

Now her face started to fall, tears pricking at her yes. Juliana was happy to leave her to her mem-ries, hopeful that she might have given the poor voman a different slant on what had clearly been n unhappy marriage. Maybe that was why Susanne ad never had children. Or maybe the not having hildren had created the unhappy marriage. Who new which came first, the chicken or the egg?

Juliana hesitated at the study door, taking a deep reath to prepare her for the fray. With both hands ull, she had to kick the door instead of knocking n it. Blake swept it open, smiling in rueful relief t her.

'Thank the lord,' he whispered.

Juliana peered over his shoulder to where Barbara vas slumped in one of the deep armchairs, her face uried in her hands. By the shaking of her body he was still weeping, though quietly. Despite her trong dislike for Blake's sister, Juliana was moved o some sympathy. Not much. But some.

'Why don't you make yourself scarce?' she uggested to her husband. 'I'll call out if I need ou.'

'You have no idea how grateful I am that you're loing this. You're a grand girl.'

'Don't thank me till later. I might just murder Barbara if she turns on me the way she used to.'

'I think you've finally turned the tables on *her*, Juliana.'

'We'll see, Blake. We'll see . . .'

Juliana allowed her husband to escape while she moved into the room with as much enthusiasm as a man going to the gallows. Barbara, she knew from experience, was not given to accepting gestures of kindness with a good grace. Blake's sister saw kindness as weakness. Juliana scooped in a breath and braced herself.

'Some coffee, Barbara?' she offered as she put the tray down on the sleekly lined grey desk.

Barbara muttered something unintelligible.

Juliana poured the coffee anyway, dropped in two cubes of sugar, stirred it thoroughly then presented it under Barbara's nose as a *fait accompli*. She waved it away with dismissive impatience.

'Blake said you were to have coffee, Barbara. So damned well take this and drink it!'

And so much for my sympathy, Juliana berated herself.

Barbara grudgingly mopped up her tears with what looked like a man's handkerchief, took the cup and saucer and started to drink, hiccuping after every mouthful.

Despite the ravages of the tears she was looking pretty good, her diet-slim body encased in a black silk dress that must have cost a king's ransom, especially with the matching coat that was draped over the back of the chair. Her hair, Juliana noted, was a more flattering shade of blonde than the last time she'd seen her, and her skin was clearly the skin of a woman who'd always had the best of facials. Barbara, at twenty-eight, was no raving beauty. But she was a classy-looking woman. No doubt about that.

'Feel like telling me what's wrong?' Juliana suggested once Blake's sister had finished the first cup and had started on the second.

'No,' Barbara pouted.

It was reminiscent of many pouts Juliana had been on the receiving-end of before. A bitter resentment welled up inside her. What in God's name was she doing, taking pity on this woman, trying to help her?

'Fair enough,' she said brusquely, standing up from where she'd been balancing on the arm-rest of a nearby chair and heading for the door. No way was she going to beg or cajole Blake's spoilt brat of a sister into womanly confidences. No way was she even going to stay around and watch her sulking.

'Where...where are you going?' Barbara wailed.

Juliana stopped, gritted her teeth, then turned slowly around. 'Upstairs to my room. It's been a long day and I'd like to change.'

'But Blake said...I know he asked you to...to...'

'To what? Listen to your problems? Give you advice? Let's be honest, Barbara—you don't want my advice. You can't stand me any more than I can stand you. This was a hopeless idea of Blake's from the start. Tell *him* your problems. I can't deal with them, or you.'

'Please don't go,' she cried out with such desperation that Juliana hesitated. 'Blake won't understand and I...I don't know what to do. Henry's cut off all my credit cards. He...he says he doesn't care where I go or what I do as long as he doesn't have to pay for it.'

'And why is he acting like this? Don't go telling me he doesn't love you, Barbara. The man loves you to distraction.'

'Because he's a jealous old fool!' Barbara burst out. 'He thinks I'm having affairs behind his back.'

'And are you?'

Barbara looked uncomfortable for once in her life. 'Not really affairs...'

'But there have been other men.'

'Well, of course there've been other men! Do you honestly think I could go my whole life only sleeping with that old coot?'

Juliana sighed. 'So you *did* only marry Henry for his money.'

'Don't you come the high horse with me, Juliana. You're not so lily-white yourself. If ever there was a girl who's always had her eye on the main chance then it's you!' She wiped her nose again and gave Juliana one of those supercilious, scoffing looks she specialised in. 'You weren't exactly in love with Blake when you married him, were you? Good God, you were engaged to another man a couple of weeks beforehand! So don't you start looking down your nose at my marriage, madam. You married my brother for his money and don't think everyone doesn't know it!'

Juliana sucked in a hurt breath for a second till she decided not to let this woman do what she had always done: make her feel rotten. *She* knew she hadn't married Blake for his money, and that was all that mattered. Having re-gathered her composure, she eyed Blake's sister with a mixture of contempt and pity. The woman really was a pathetic creature.

'Don't presume to judge my marriage, Barbara,' she said with as much forbearance as she could muster. 'Or the reasons behind it. Blake and I are a very special case.'

'Oh, I don't doubt that! You and he were always as thick as thieves, even when you were kids. And so secretive! All those afternoons you used to spend in his room,' she sneered. 'I mean, girls like you start young, don't they?'

Now Juliana had heard enough. There was a limit to everything. 'Get out,' she said quite calmly.

'W-what?'

'You heard me. Get out. Right now.' Striding over, she swept the coat up from the back of the chair and threw it at the open-mouthed woman.

Barbara got unsteadily to her feet. 'You have no r-right to do this. Blake . . . Blake said I could stay till I s-sorted myself out.'

'He will retract that once I've told him what you just said. Now *move*!'

'I will not!' she resisted stubbornly. 'I have a right to stay here if I want to. This is my *home*.'

'You left this home when you married,' Juliana pointed out icily. '*I* am mistress of this house now.'

Barbara's upper lip curled in open contempt. 'Too true, you little slut. That's all you are. All you'll ever be to my brother. His mistress! Oh, you might have a marriage certificate, but he never wanted you as his wife! All you are is a legitimised whore! Blake will never want any woman other than sexually. Darling Mummy screwed him up good and proper. And what she didn't screw up, darling Daddy did!'

Her laughter was quite lewd. 'Speaking of screwing, I'll bet you never guessed who was one of the many *ladies* Daddy was having on the side, did you? Oh, I see it's dawning on you. Yes, your own darling mother. Our own sweetly caring cook, Lily! Don't look so shocked, Juliana, dear. You couldn't have been ignorant of your mother's appetite for sex. Like mother, like daughter, eh, what? *You* certainly must be good at it for Blake to marry you. He always told me he'd only ever marry for money. That's why he dumped poor old Virginia as soon as he found out she was flat chat. Yet he married you!'

She smiled an ugly smile as she slipped into her coat. 'I guess some habits die hard. Maybe he decided to install a nice regular bedmate for him to have between trips overseas. Yes, that must be it. He has his little black book full of international good-time girls to cater for him while he's away and good old reliable Juliana to fix him up at home, the way she always did.'

Juliana grimaced as she gulped down the rising nausea in her throat. Her head began to whirl.

It wasn't true. Mum couldn't have been sleeping with Matthew Preston. She would have known it if she were!

But, even as she denied it to herself, Juliana remembered the cigar smoke she used to smell when she came home from school. Matthew Preston had smoked cigars.

As for Barbara's accusation about Blake and other women overseas...

Juliana swallowed again, then lifted her chin proudly. 'I don't believe a word you've just said, Barbara. You're a jealous, vindictive bitch. You've always been a jealous, vindictive bitch. In your hate for me you don't even care if you ruin your own brother's happiness. For we *are* happy. I know that won't go down too well with you, since you've made such a mess of your own life. Not that I give a damn about that! Blake always told me people got their come-uppance. I didn't believe him before. Now I do. You've made your bed, Barbara. Go home and lie in it. Meanwhile, I'm quite happy to lie in mine, with Blake by my side. He cares about me. Whether you believe that or not is immaterial. *I* do. And he does not sleep around!'

Barbara laughed. 'Really! Well, why don't you check out the top drawer on the left-hand bedside chest in his room? That's where he keeps his little black book. You'll find all the women in it plus their phone numbers. I dare you to have a look tonight before you curl up in your cosy little bed. Maybe you won't be so smug then. Maybe you'll realise exactly what you are to Blake. Why, you're

no more to him than your mother was to my
f——'

Juliana slapped Barbara's face so hard that the
sound reverberated in the room. Or was that
Barbara's scream?

She would have slapped her again if Blake hadn't
raced into the room.

'What in God's name is going on in here?' he
demanded to know.

'Barbara is just leaving,' Juliana said with
stunning outward calm. 'Aren't you?'

Barbara was staring at her, frightened perhaps
by the look in her sister-in-law's eyes.

'And she won't be coming back,' Juliana
finished.

Blake looked first at his pale-faced wife, then at
his defiant sister. For a long moment the air tingled
with electric tension. Which way would his loyalty
go?

Finally, he turned to Barbara with a hardening
expression. 'I don't know what you've just said to
Juliana, but if it's what I think it is I'm going to
strangle you with my bare hands.'

For the first time, Barbara looked worried, then
she became aggressively defensive. 'What *I* said to
her? You should have heard what *she* said to *me*!
Called me a bitch, told me I had made my bed and
now I had to lie in it. She's cruel and horrible,
Blake. I don't know why you married her. You
didn't *have* to marry her to get what you wanted,
you know. She would have been as easy as her...'

She gasped as she realised she'd really put her
foot in her mouth.

'You have five seconds to get out of here,' Blake said in a low, steady voice that was infinitely terrifying. 'Out! Don't walk. Run! As fast as you can or I won't be responsible for what happens to you.'

Panic-stricken now, Barbara glanced from one to the other, then, with a sob, ran from the room. They heard her high heels clack hurriedly across the marble foyer, heard the front door bang.

'Juliana,' Blake said thickly, and gathered her into his arms.

She went, collapsing, unable to think of anything but what he'd just confirmed with his action. Her mother *had* been his father's lover, had perhaps contributed to his mother's suicide. It was all so appalling, so... shattering.

'I... I never knew,' she sobbed. 'I never knew...'

'Hush, my darling. Hush. It's all in the past and quite inconsequential now. There's nothing to feel too terrible about.'

Juliana struggled out of his arms, tears streaming down her face. 'Nothing too terrible? Good God, how can you say that? My own mother was responsible for your mother's death!'

'No...' Blake shook his head. 'She never knew about Father and Lily. I swear to you. They hid it very well. I only found out quite by accident when I came home unexpectedly from university one night and saw Dad slipping down the back stairs from your flat. He only had trousers on. It didn't take much to put two and two together. I knew Dad had been having affairs for years.'

Juliana stared at him. 'You're talking about the night of my graduation, aren't you?'

Blake sighed. 'Yes.'

'Oh, God...' She pressed her fingers against her throbbing temples. 'How you must have despised him. And my mother!'

'I never despised Lily, Juliana. She was the nicest woman I ever knew, but she was also lonely and vulnerable. My father was a handsome, charming, sophisticated man. She didn't stand a chance against him. As for my father...I didn't despise him either. I knew what he was, knew he had this weakness for warm, beautiful, giving women like your mother. Sure, I was disillusioned for a while. What son doesn't want his father to be a paragon of perfection? And the young do judge harshly. But eventually I understood why he craved escape from my mother's relentless jealousy and possessiveness. Women like that make men want to run, and run and run. They kill all that's good in a relationship. They make loving anyone a living hell!'

'Which is why you've never loved anyone,' Juliana said, and looked away. 'Nor wanted them to love you.'

'I certainly don't want that kind of love. But I do want *you*, Juliana. I have ever since you were thirteen.'

Her eyes snapped back, rounding with shock.

His own expression was self-mocking. 'Remember that day by the pool when you felt my muscles?'

She nodded, her mouth dry.

'I wanted to grab you then, kiss you, force you. I was a virgin myself, would you believe it, but it was your virginity on the line that day, Juliana. It took every ounce of my control to dive into that pool and swim away from you.'

'I...I had no idea...'

'Do you think I didn't realise that? You were still a child, despite your rapidly growing body. But I was nineteen, and a nineteen-year-old boy's desires are very strong. Still, I soon found a remedy,' he finished almost bitterly.

Juliana was silent for a few seconds.

'I...I was very jealous of all those girls,' she said softly.

Blake smiled. 'Were you? I'm glad.'

'Glad?'

'Glad that you suffered as much as I was suffering.'

'You weren't suffering, Blake Preston! You were having the time of your life!'

'Was I? Oh, Juliana, if only you knew...I used to watch and wait for you every time I came home from university just to catch a glimpse of you, to marvel at the way nature was turning you into such a beauty. I kept thinking to myself, Soon...soon she'll be sixteen, soon she'll be at the age of consent...'

Juliana was startled. 'You...you planned to seduce me when I turned sixteen?'

'Do you want me to deny it?'

'Well...no, I suppose not. Not if it's true.' Yet she did feel somewhat dismayed at the thought.

'Good lord, Juliana, I was a spoilt, sex-crazed rich kid who thought he could have any girl he wanted. Believe me when I say I had never been knocked back. Yet the only girl I really wanted was you, probably because you were forbidden; a challenge. Why do you think I came home early from university that night? I couldn't wait another day to see you. I had no idea that was the night of your graduation ball. I thought, it being a Wednesday, you'd be home. Then there was my father, coming down from a rendezvous with your mother.'

His laugh was derisive. 'Seeing him changed everything. Oh, I still wanted you. I might even have seduced you that night if you'd let me. But you didn't, Juliana. You told me off and made me see reality, which was that we could never be happy together while my father was having an affair with your mother. It was an impossible situation. As much as I tried telling myself that I could still have you if I wanted you, I couldn't bear to see the look in Lily's eyes when and if she found out both she and her daughter had been ill-used by Preston men. I also thought it was only a matter of time before *you* found out about them. But you never did.'

'No, I never did,' she murmured, still astounded by all that Blake had told her. She had no idea she'd been the object of such a long sexual obsession. He'd certainly hidden it very well. There again, she'd hidden her own love for just as long, even from herself.

'Barbara only knew because I told her one night in a drunken binge shortly after Dad's death.'

'I'm surprised she didn't tell me sooner,' Juliana said with a catch in her voice.

'I warned her not to.' Blake gathered her still shaken self back into his arms, laying her head on his shoulder. 'I never dreamt she would come out with it at this late stage. I'm sorry, Juliana. I won't let her hurt you again. I promise.'

'She's always hated me.'

'No, she's always *envied* you. Your beauty; your honesty; your love of life.'

'I don't love life very much tonight.'

'You will. I'm going to make you forget Barbara, and the past. I'm going to make you forget everything, Juliana, but here and now.' And, tipping up her chin, he kissed her with such passion that she was well on the way to forgetting before they left the room.

CHAPTER TEN

JULIANA woke the next morning, once again in Blake's bed. His side was empty, the bedside clock said seven-fifteen and his shower was running.

Friday, she thought. And groaned. Friday was not her favourite day at work. The sales teams came in for their weekly meeting and she never seemed to get anything done. To tell the truth, she didn't feel like going to work at all that day. She felt tired and troubled after the happenings of the night before.

Blake had not been able to dispel all her distress over what she'd found out about her mother and his father, no matter how hard he'd tried. In fact, the more passionate he became, the more perturbed she felt underneath, about a whole lot of things, the main one being what exactly did she mean to Blake? Was Barbara right? Was she no better than a legitimised mistress?

Juliana breathed in sharply. Oh, my God, the book... The little black book. That was one thing she *had* forgotten about.

She stared at the top left-hand-side drawer, then at the bathroom door. The shower was still running strongly. Dared she look?

And what if the book was there, with a whole lot of women's names and phone numbers in it? What would that prove? It did not mean Blake was still using either the book, or the women. He might simply not have thrown the rotten darned thing away after they were married.

Her stomach twisted. The urge to know if it was there, a reality, and not another one of Barbara's malicious inventions, was compelling.

I won't look inside, Juliana vowed. I just want to know if it exists.

Her hand trembled as it reached for the knob on the drawer, but there was no turning back now. The decision had been made.

She yanked it open.

Three neat piles of various coloured handkerchiefs greeted her, behind which lay a battered copy of *The Power of One*. Peeping out from under the novel was the corner of—not a little black book—but a little dark blue one.

Juliana frowned. Was this it?

There was only one way to find out.

Holding her breath, she eased the small leatherbound note book out from under its hiding spot. As she started to flick through it, her heart began to thud. Her fingers slowed. Her eyes widened.

Each successive page revealed a stunning array of women's names and numbers, listed under the city they lived in. Jennifer in London; Simone in Paris; Carla in Italy; Maria in Greece; Ellie in Bangkok; Jasmine in Hong Kong; Midori in Tokyo; Cindy in New York.

And that was only a sample.

The list was staggering. There were even some interstate numbers. Girls in Sydney and Brisbane and Canberra and Adelaide and Perth.

The sudden snapping off of the shower sent
Juliana into a panic. Shoving the book back, she
banged the drawer shut and dived back under the
sheets. With some difficulty she resisted the silly
urge to pretend she was still asleep when Blake came
back into the room, a towel slung low around his
hips.

'You still in bed?' He smiled wryly and walked
across the room to fling open his wardrobe, well
aware, Juliana thought despairingly, of how incredibly sexy he looked like that. His daily twenty
laps in the pool, plus all his other sporting activities kept his broad-shouldered, slim-hipped frame
in top condition. The skiing in winter, the tennis in
summer, not to mention the odd hit of squash and
the occasional game of golf, all kept the fat away
and those gold-skinned muscles well-toned and
rippling.

'You're going to be late for work if you don't
get up,' he remarked as he dropped the towel and
casually drew on brief black underpants.

'I . . . I think I'll take a sickie.'

This brought a sharp glance over his shoulder.
'That's not like you. Aren't you feeling well this
morning? Your period's not due today, is it?'

'You know damned well it isn't,' she snapped
before she could stop herself.

Blake frowned at her for a moment, then with a
casual shrug turned back and kept on dressing.

Juliana watched him with a gradual sickening in
her stomach. He was so beautiful, yet perhaps so
frighteningly amoral. His dark suspicions over *her*
having an affair probably reflected the fact that he

was having them himself, right, left and centre. Men were renowned for their double set of standards where sex was concerned. And it wasn't as though Blake's father had set him a good example . . .

Juliana cringed inside again to think of what had been going on under her nose all those years. Not that she blamed her mother—Blake was right about that. A woman of her nature and susceptibility to men wouldn't have stood a chance against a man like Matthew Preston. Any woman would have found him hard to resist. Lily would have been putty in his hands.

Just as I am putty in Blake's hands, Juliana thought with a growing sense of despair. He hasn't fallen in love with me. He only *wants* me. I've been fooling myself where that's concerned. Oh, maybe he almost meant it when he said there would never be another woman for him. The women in those books probably weren't *women* to him. They were merely bodies. There were too many of them to be anything else.

Weren't?

Who said they were in the past tense? Juliana mocked herself. They could be well and truly present, *and* future.

Still, the lingering hope that Blake no longer used that little book and would not have any need to use it in future revived her naturally optimistic nature. She could cope with Blake's not loving her if he didn't cheat on her. And really, she had no evidence of any actual cheating. The book's existence proved nothing. Barbara's knowledge of it actually proved that Blake had had that book for years!

'Do you want me to ring your office for you?' he offered as he tucked a white shirt into his pin-striped navy trousers.

Suddenly the prospect of moping around the house all day, worrying about everything, was too awful to contemplate. What could she achieve by it, except get herself into more of a mental and emotional muddle?

'No, thanks,' she told him. 'No need. I've decided to go in after all. I'll just have to be a little late.'

'I'll say. You usually take ages getting ready. Well, I'm off downstairs for breakfast. See you tonight.' He came over and pecked her on the forehead. 'Don't forget, we've got that dinner-party at Jack's tonight.'

Juliana pulled a face. 'I had forgotten. Oh, well . . . It won't be too bad, I suppose. Jack's good fun, and I do want to thank him personally for those tickets to *Phantom*.'

Blake patted her cheek. 'That's my girl.'

Juliana's heart sank as she watched her husband stride confidently from the room, putting on his suit jacket on the way. He was already in his business mode, his bed and its occupant quite forgotten.

There would be no inner turmoil while *he* sat at his desk that day, no more worries over his wife's loyalty. He had her now in the palm of his hand. And how he knew it! She would be ready and waiting for him when he came home tonight, both for the dinner-party and any other party he might want afterwards.

Juliana swallowed at this thought. Blake had certainly turned her heightened sexuality to his advantage. He seemed to be enjoying the power he now had over her in bed to have her do whatever he desired, to reduce her to a wildly willing partner who didn't know the words 'no' or 'stop' or 'don't'. Not that she could blame him, she supposed. What man didn't want a woman to be his sexual slave? And what woman didn't want her man to be as skilled and imaginative as Blake was? The situation was a double-edged sword all right.

With a sigh Juliana climbed from the bed, gathered her clothes up from where they were scattered over the floor and made her way slowly back to her room. She wished she could be really happy about the way things were going in her marriage; wished she could dismiss all thought of that infernal notebook. But she knew its existence would be a constant thorn in her side. She also knew that the next time Blake went away on business she would be sorely tempted to see if he had left it behind or taken it with him.

He left it behind, and she was ecstatic.

The occasion was the last week in November. And, while Blake was only away three short days in Hong Kong, the days leading up to his trip had been the wrong time of the month for Juliana, and she figured if Blake was ever going to be suspect it might be after he'd been deprived of sex for a while.

Juliana hadn't dragged up the courage to actually look in the drawer till the very evening Blake was due back. She felt so elated at finding that book still in its hidey-hole that she impulsively decided to go and meet him at the airport, despite there being barely enough time for her to make it by the time Blake's plane touched down shortly after nine o'clock.

Some impulses, she realised after she saw Stewart Margin's reaction to her last-minute appearance, were not such a good idea. Blake's secretary was sitting in the waiting lounge next to Gate Three, his nose buried in a newspaper, when she stepped from the moving walkway and hurried over.

'Hello, Stewart,' she said, quite happily at that stage.

His eyes snapped up, his face showing instant alarm. 'Mrs Preston!' He shut the newspaper noisily and scrambled to his feet. 'What...what are *you* doing here?'

'Just thought I'd come along and meet my husband.'

'Does—er—Mr Preston know you're meeting him?'

'No. Why? Is he late again?'

'No. His plane's already landed. It's just that...well—um——' He shrugged uncomfortably, looking as though he wished he were anywhere else but here.

Juliana started wishing the same. She shouldn't have come. It had been a stupid thing to do. Naïve and stupid.

Her earlier elation died. How could she have believed Blake would be pleased she was here, waiting for him like an adoring little wife? Their relationship might have changed, but not *that* much. Just because they now slept together in his bed every night, all night, it did not mean he would want her fawning all over him in public.

Stewart's muttering something under his breath added another dimension to Juliana's dismay. Dear heaven, surely Blake wouldn't start thinking things, because she was here with Stewart, would he?

Though not having openly continued with his crazy accusation about her having had an affair the last time he'd been away, Blake *had* become more possessive—even watchful—over her. When Jack had mildly flirted with her the night of his and Gloria's dinner-party, Blake had glared at his host with a withering coldness.

On one other occasion he'd questioned her rather sharply when she'd been very late home from work. Half-flattered, half-frustrated, Juliana had impatiently explained that she'd left the office on time, but had been caught in a traffic jam. Blake's considered and very chilly silence for several minutes afterwards had given her the disquieting feeling that he hadn't believed her.

A premonition of impending doom swept through her.

She might have turned and fled if passengers hadn't started filing from the flight tunnel into the lounge where she and Stewart were standing. Blake was the third person along, his blue eyes narrowing when he saw them both together.

Juliana gulped, plastered a bright smile on her face and determined not to let her inner disquiet show. After all, she *was* innocent.

'What are you doing here, Juliana?' were Blake's first words. His tone was measured. Not exactly accusing, but definitely not happy.

'I couldn't wait to see you,' she said, truthfully enough. And, stepping forward, she held him by the shoulders while she kissed him on the cheek. His body felt stiff beneath her hands, his skin coldly unwelcome.

She drew back, her smile strained now.

'How nice,' was his flat reply. 'How did you get here? You always said you'd never drive at night in the city.'

'I caught a taxi.'

'You should have asked Stewart to drive you. After all, you did know he would be meeting me, didn't you?'

Juliana could feel her discomfort developing into a fully fledged fluster. 'Well, yes, I did, but I—er— it was a last-minute decision to come...'

'Oh?' His smile was blackly sardonic. 'Was it quicker to come here than go home?'

Stewart, Juliana knew, lived in the northern suburbs of Melbourne, a long way from their bayside home.

An angry exasperation cooled her embarrassing blush. She straightened her shoulders and gave Blake a reproachful look. 'No,' was all she said, determined not to be verbally bullied like this. Hopefully Blake's nasty innuendoes were going over poor Stewart's head, though from the look of the young man's obvious agitation she didn't think so.

Truly, Blake was being unforgivably horrible. Yet there she'd been, less than half an hour ago, dying for him to go home. Now she felt absolutely wretched.

Blake at last acknowledged his secretary's presence. 'Hello, Stewart. Everything all right here while I was away?'

'A few small problems, Mr Preston. Nothing I couldn't handle.'

'Where are we parked?'

'The usual spot.'

'Fine. Let's go, then. Sorry, Juliana, but Stewart and I will be talking shop during the drive home. I hope you don't mind sitting in the back on your own, but, let's face it, neither of us had any idea you'd be here, did we, Stewart?'

'We certainly didn't,' the secretary agreed quite forcefully.

'I don't mind,' she said, as civilly as her fury would allow. Never again, she vowed. Never again!

It began to drizzle on the way home, the temperature dropping as well. No one, other than Melbournians, would have dreamt summer was only two days away. Dressed only in lightweight forest-green casual trousers and a cream silk blouse, Juliana hugged herself in the back seat of the company Ford, wishing Stewart would turn on the heater. He didn't, and she stubbornly refused to ask.

She glared, first at the back of Blake's head, then out at the rain-spattered pavements, her nerves stretched to breaking-point by the time Stewart dropped them off at the house. She wasn't sure which of them was going to snap first, but it was obvious, by the tension between them as they went inside, that a fight was brewing.

In a way, Juliana would have appreciated the chance to clear the air, but Blake, it seemed, was content to let silence be his weapon. After delivering his luggage to Mrs Dawson for her to do his washing, he strode into the living-room to pour himself his usual nightcap. Juliana trailed after him, strung up and irritated. She wandered around the room while Blake downed a very stiff drink, then poured himself another. Not a word had passed between them. Suddenly, it was too much for her and she whirled on him.

'Don't you ever do that to me again!' she burst out.

'Do what?' he returned blandly.

'You know what, Blake. Don't play the innocent with me.'

His laughter was bitter. 'I thought that was my line.'

'See? You're doing it again. Making nasty innuendoes.'

'Is that what I'm doing?' He quaffed back half the second whisky then topped up the glass.

'You know that's what you're doing. And it's so unfair. I have never been unfaithful to you. Not the last time you were away, nor this time!'

'Is that so?'

'Yes, that's so!'

'In that case you won't mind coming upstairs with me now, will you?' He turned and stared at her over the rim of his glass while he drank. His gaze was hard and cold, yet appallingly sexual. Juliana felt her skin begin to crawl with a ghastly excitement. 'I feel like making love to my wife.'

He placed the empty glass on to the coffee-table with a clunk, then began to walk towards the door. Checking mid-stride halfway across the room, he turned to eye her still standing there. 'Aren't you coming, darling?' he asked in a softly mocking tone. 'A faithful wife who is so anxious for her husband to come home that she meets him breathlessly at the airport must surely be in need of a little loving.'

He held out his hand to her.

She stared at it for a long moment, then slowly lifted her eyes to his.

'Yes, Blake,' she said, her heart breaking. 'I am. But that's not what you're offering, is it? What *you're* offering I can get in *any* man's bedroom.'

She could see that she had stunned him with her counter-attack. Stunned and infuriated him.

'I don't doubt it. You've become quite the little sensualist lately, haven't you?'

'And that bothers you?'

For a second, his nostrils flared, his eyes glittering angrily. But he quickly gathered himself. 'Why should it? Do you think I was *happy* with our previous sex-life? Good God!'

Juliana looked away from his scathing contempt. '*I* was,' she said brokenly.

He scoffed his disbelief.

'At the time,' she added, her gaze returning to his.

'And what happened to change all that, if you don't mind my asking for the umpteenth time?'

She simply stared at him, unable to think of a reason other than the truth. And she couldn't tell him that.

He started walking slowly towards her. 'Cat got your tongue, Juliana? Shall I fill in the blanks for you?'

He stopped right in front of her, his face mocking. 'I know exactly what happened,' he said in a low, dark voice. 'You met some bastard, some wicked, clever bastard who took no notice of your ice-princess routine, who took no notice of your prudish little ways, who simply *took*!'

His hands were busy on her blouse as he spoke, unflicking the buttons, parting the material so that he could easily unsnap the front fastening of her bra. His eyes darkened as they swept over the rosy tips, already hard with arousal.

'You found out you liked it that way, didn't you? Nothing too gentle or sweet for this new Juliana...' And his hands started putting his words into actions.

She bit her bottom lip to stop any sound from escaping, her eyes pained when he bent to replace his hands with an even less gentle mouth. The appalling thought that Susanne could come into the room at any moment only seemed to add to her excitement. And her shame.

The shame finally escalated when his hands went to the waistband of her trousers.

'No...' she said shakily, and staggered backwards, fumbling as she did some of the buttons back up. 'No!' she cried. 'You're wrong. About me. About everything! It...it wasn't like that. I'm not like that. Oh, I can't stand this any more. I can't stand it, I tell you. I have to get out of here, away from you. I . . . I have to . . .'

She left him, standing there with his jaw dropped open. She didn't stop to pick up her bag, just swept her car keys from where they hung on a peg on the kitchen wall and raced for the garage. Susanne, luckily, was nowhere in sight. No doubt she was busy washing in the laundry or watching television in the family room.

Pressing the remote-control panel that opened the garage door and the front gate, Juliana leapt into her car and fired the engine. Blake must have thought she'd run upstairs, for he hadn't followed her into the garage. It wasn't till she was roaring up the street that her rear-view mirror caught him racing out on to the wet pavement, waving his arms at her to stop.

But she did not stop, and after a couple of intersections she knew he wouldn't be able to find her. She swept the small sedan up several side-streets and screeched to a halt in a dark lane, only then realising she was shaking like a leaf.

Slumping across the steering-wheel, she started to cry. And once she started she could not stop.

Finally, she was all cried out, but the weeping, she found, had not solved anything. It simply left her drained of every ounce of strength, both physically and emotionally. There was no energy left, no fight, no will. She really could not go on. She also could not go home. Not yet. No . . . certainly not yet . . .

Like an automaton, she started up the car and drove slowly, aimlessly. Somehow she found herself going towards the city on the road she usually took to go to work, the water on her left, houses on her right. Swinging round a curve she spotted St Kilda pier in the distance stretching out into the grey waters of the bay.

Juliana remembered how, as a teenager, she'd often spent hours walking along that pier, idly watching the horizon or the student artists who used to sit there, painting the boats. It had been a type of refuge for her whenever she'd been troubled in some way. Usually, by the time she left the pier, things had seemed more in perspective. Less catastrophic. The water, it seemed, had had a soothing, calming effect.

Despite the late hour, she pulled over and parked in one of the parking bays across from the pier, making her way over via the arched walkway that spanned the busy road. Down the steps she went and along on to the pier proper.

Practically deserted, the place was, yet she didn't find it creepy. There was one man—a drunk by the look of him—leaning on one of the posts, and further along a lone fisherman was trying his luck. The rain had temporarily stopped and a faint moon was shining through the clouds. The water looked pretty black, but still peaceful.

Juliana walked over to a private spot and leant against the railing to peer blankly out to sea. The water lapped softly around the posts underneath her pier. Moored boats rocked gently in front of her. Gradually, a peace stole over her tormented soul. Yes, she'd been right to stop here.

She was standing there, reviving her spirits and the will to go on with her marriage, when something hit her on the back of the head.

CHAPTER ELEVEN

'SHE'S coming round...'

Juliana moaned again when some person—a doctor, presumably—pulled up successive eyelids and shone a bright light into each eye. She lifted an uncoordinated hand to push the pencil-thin torch away.

'Hi, there, Mrs Preston. I'm Dr Trumbole. How are you feeling?'

'My... my head aches,' she managed to get out, her voice sounding slurred.

'I'm sure it does. But don't worry. You've got a nasty bump on the back of your head and a mild concussion, but you'll live.' He smiled down at her. 'I'll get the nurse to give you something for the headache.'

'How long does my wife have to stay in hospital?' Blake asked from where he was standing at the foot of the bed, looking almost as bad as Juliana was feeling.

'We'll keep her in for another day, just as a precautionary measure.'

'So she might be able to go home tomorrow?'

'I don't see why not, provided she can go home to nothing but strict bed-rest for several days. No work of any kind. She shouldn't even walk around much. I trust that won't be a problem?'

'She won't lift a finger.'

168

'Good. I must go and start my rounds. The nurse will be back shortly with some tablets for you, Mrs Preston. Now don't worry if you feel sleepy soon after taking them. They'll contain a sedative as well. Goodbye, Mr Preston.'

'Goodbye, and ... thank you, Doctor. You've been most kind.'

The doctor patted Blake's shoulder. 'Someone had to reassure you that your wife was not going to die.'

Once they were alone Blake came forward to sit on the side of the bed, picking up her hand between his. His sigh was weary. 'God, Juliana, don't ever do anything like that again. You had me so darned worried. When you didn't come home all night I rang the police. They told me you answered the description of an unconscious lady found on St Kilda pier. Apparently some old bum contacted them about you but he'd done a flit by the time they and the ambulance arrived. Since you had no ID on you, they had no idea who you were.'

As she stared at his grim expression, a horrible thought came to mind, making her stomach churn. 'Blake, I wasn't ... I mean ... whoever attacked me ... he didn't ... didn't ...'

'No, no. He didn't touch you other than to hit you. From what the police have gathered he just took your keys and stole your car. Must have followed you from where you'd parked it. They've already located the car, stripped and burnt out in a park somewhere.'

Tears pricked at her eyes. 'My poor little car ...'

'I'll buy you another car.'

A type of resentment welled up at his offer. Di
he think he could solve every problem that easily
Just whip out his chequebook? Well, it would tak
more than money to erase the memory of last night
Much more than money...

'No, Blake. I'll buy my own car.'

He dropped her hand and stood up, exasperatio
on his face. 'For pity's sake, Juliana, would it hur
you to let me buy you a damned car? There's
limit to independence, you know, especially for
man's wife!'

She just looked at him, not having the energy t
argue. Eventually, he let out a disgruntled sigh an
sat back down. But he didn't pick up her han
again.

'All right, all right, I'm being irrational,' he ad
mitted. 'But I feel so rotten about last night. I acte
like a pig out at the airport. Then, when we go
home, I treated you abominably. There was n
excuse for what I did. I hope you will accept m
apology, Juliana. I assure you nothing like that wil
ever happen again.'

He'd barely finished his stiffly formal and no
really appeasing words when the ward sister bustle
in with a glass of water and two huge whit
capsules.

'Here we are, Mrs Preston. If these don't shif
your headache, nothing can. Only problem i
getting them down. Drink plenty of water wit
them. Here... let me help you sit up.'

Juliana gulped the bombs down, lying back
afterwards with a ragged groan. Her head wa
killing her.

'Poor dear,' the sister soothed, and straightened the bedclothes. 'You'll feel better soon. Did the doctor tell you you'd probably drift off to sleep?'

She nodded.

'Nice nurse, that,' Blake remarked after she left.

'Mmm.'

'I'll go once you get sleepy.'

'All right.'

A heavy silence descended. Juliana was in too much pain to make idle chit-chat, let alone tackle the problems that still beset their personal relationship. Blake's apology did not alter the fact that, underneath, he believed she was an adulteress. Maybe he thought he would now magnanimously push this belief to the back of his mind, but Juliana knew it would lurk there, poisoning what could have been so good between them.

How could she happily go to his bed knowing he thought she'd done all those intimate things with some other man—or men? And what of Blake, being prepared to sleep with a wife he thought was a two-timing tramp? What did that make her, if not what Barbara had accused her of being? Blake's legal whore...

Juliana's heart sank to an all-time low. She might have wept if her aching eyes and whirling head hadn't started feeling so heavy. A yawn captured her mouth. She closed her eyes.

Though almost asleep, she flinched slightly when she felt Blake's lips on her forehead.

She thought she heard a sigh. Was it hers, or his? She didn't hear him leave the room at all. By then, the sedative had done its work.

*   *   *

Juliana did go home the next day, despite sti'
feeling exhausted. Though maybe it was more a'
emotional exhaustion than a physical one
Depression had taken its hold and she could no
seem to throw it off.

Susanne, perhaps sensing that all was not wel'
with her, fussed like an old mother hen. Nothin,
was too much trouble. A television and video wer
set up in Juliana's bedroom. Piles of books wer
collected from the local library. Magazines ap
peared in droves, donated by Susanne's sister.

Juliana was only allowed out of bed to showe
or to go to the bathroom. Her own local docto
visited daily to check on her progress. Vitamins wer
prescribed along with tablets that looked sus
piciously like tranquillisers. Juliana flushed then
down the toilet. Flowers arrived in abundance fron
people she worked with, with a couple of the girl
dropping by regularly for visits after work, bringin,
good cheer, chocolates, fruit and more magazines

But, despite everything, Juliana remaine
depressed.

Blake, of course, was the reason. Juliana woul
have liked to talk to him about their relationship
Really talked in a deep and meaningful way. Bu
he was so unapproachable in his manner and atti
tude that it was impossible.

Though superficially kind and considerate, h
began treating her more like a distant invalid relativ
than a wife. She felt he did what he did throug
duty, not true caring, their meetings awkwar
and strained.

He would stop by briefly in the morning for a few moments' stiff conversation before breakfast, telephone her once during the day with a couple of brisk questions about how she was feeling, then condescend to eat his meal with her in her room at night, though he silently watched the news on the television while they ate. He also suddenly seemed to have to retire to his study every evening after dinner to work or make phone calls. There was certainly no question of his ever coming into her bed at night, not even just to hold her or be with her.

Juliana began to fear that Blake was using the situation to regress to their earlier separate-bedrooms, separate-lives status. And, while she didn't want to be used like some whore, the intimacy of sex might have broken down the emotional barriers Blake seemed to be re-erecting. But making love never came up in their meagre conversations, though admittedly the doctor might have told Blake that was out for a while. She was lucky if she got a peck goodnight, let alone a hug or a proper kiss.

It depressed Juliana further to think that if Blake couldn't actually sleep with her he didn't want to touch her at all. Was that marriage?

Well, they had never had a real marriage, she decided unhappily, and it had taken this crisis to show up the weaknesses in their relationship. Yet she had once deluded herself into thinking that their marriage was strong. How crazy could one get?

But of course that had been before she'd realised she loved Blake, before she'd started wanting so much more than her husband had been prepared to give. Well, she *had* got more, in a physical sense, but Juliana was gradually coming to the conclusion that, even if they resumed their sex-life, their marriage was still doomed to failure. It was like a time bomb ticking away, waiting to self-destruct. Her problem now was, did she want to wait for the time bomb to explode, or take her future into her own hands and walk away with her self-respect and pride intact?

When Saturday came and Blake still went into the office, Juliana almost despaired.

'I can't take much more of this,' she muttered to herself, and, throwing hack the covers, she drew on her old pink dressing-gown and slowly made her way downstairs.

Susanne was busily polishing the foyer floor when she looked up and saw Juliana. 'You're not supposed to be coming down here,' she scolded. 'The doctor said maybe tomorrow you could sit by the pool in the sunshine. Tomorrow is not today. And you don't even have slippers on! Oh, truly, Juliana, do you want to catch your death of cold?'

'You sound just like my mother used to,' Juliana said, a lump forming in her throat. 'She . . . she was the cook here, did you know that?'

The housekeeper looked up at her with real surprise. 'No . . . no, I didn't know that.'

Juliana traced her hand over the elegantly carved knob at the end of the balustrade, a knot in her stomach. 'I'm not really cut out to be the lady of the house, I suppose. I should have known it wouldn't work . . .'

'Juliana, what are you talking about? You're one of the nicest ladies I've ever worked for. Why

ou're a *real* lady, not like some of those stuck-up
nadams who think money has given them class.
All I can say is, your mother must have been a real
ady too, because you're a credit to her. Don't ever
et me hear you putting yourself down again, do
ou hear me?'

Juliana blinked her shock at the other woman's
giving her a right dressing-down. But maybe that
vas what she needed to jolt her out of this crip-
oling depression.

'And another thing,' the housekeeper raved on,
ner face flushed with emotion. 'I think that after
Christmas you and Mr Preston should plan a little
noliday away together. If my Fred and I had spent
nore time alone together we would have been a lot
nappier. Your Mr Preston works too hard. And so
lo you. There comes a time, you know, when if a
couple don't have a baby it gets too late. They drift
apart and everything becomes just awful.'

She stepped forward and touched Juliana com-
passionately on the sleeve. 'Now I know how much
ou love that handsome husband of yours. My
neart almost breaks with the way you look at him
sometimes, but there's no use thinking *you* can
change his cold little ways. Mr Preston is one of
hose men who doesn't want to appear weak in front
of a woman. But put his own flesh and blood in
nis arms, and he'll melt to mush. I'll bet my lotto
noney on it!'

Juliana stared at the other woman.

A baby...Blake had asked her to have a baby.
But she hadn't been prepared to take the risk.

But loving someone was always a risk, and sh
prided herself on not being a coward.

Tears of gratitude filled her eyes as she looke
at this stern-faced but kindly woman whom, till re
cently, Juliana had held at arm's length. 'You coul
be right. Yes, you could be right. I'll discuss
second honeymoon with Blake when he come
home. Thank you, Susanne. I feel much bette
now.'

But she didn't really get the chance to discuss
second honeymoon with Blake. He came into he
bedroom late that afternoon with a big cardboar
box in his arms, 'Hello, there,' he greeted. 'You'r
looking much better.'

She put her book down with a ready smile, re
membering her new resolve not to give up on thi
marriage till she had fired every bullet she had. '
went downstairs for a while. What have you go
there?' she asked with real curiosity in her voice
Blake was the only person who hadn't brough
presents to her sick-bed, maybe because everyon
else had inundated her with them. Of course, it wa
typical of Blake not to give presents.

'A little get-well gift,' he told her.

As he carried the box across the room, whim
pering sounds emanated from the holes in the sides

'Oh, Blake! It's a puppy, isn't it?' She clappe
delightedly. 'Show me, show me!'

'Patience!' he commanded, and placed the bo
on the bedcovers next to her, opening the lid flap
to reveal the most adorable bundle of black canin
fur she'd ever seen.

'Oh, Blake!' She swept the puppy up into her arms, whereupon it immediately started madly licking her face as if to show its gratitude at finally escaping that awful prison of darkness.

'What breed is it?' she asked.

'Labrador.'

'You're cute as a button, aren't you, darling? That's what I'm going to call him—Buttons.'

'I thought he might keep you company while I'm away.'

Juliana's eyes jerked up. Blake was looking down at the puppy with no readable expression on his face. He looked, as always, incredibly handsome in a dark grey business suit. But his handsomeness no longer mattered to Juliana. It was his heart she coveted.

'You're not going away again before Christmas, are you?' she asked with a catch in her voice.

'Have to, I'm afraid. There have been some problems with a shipment of video games. When the container ship arrived last week we only had half the stock. The best and quickest way I can sort this out is to go over there personally.'

'Over where?'

'Tokyo.'

'I . . . I see . . .'

'I don't want to go, Juliana. I have to.'

'Of course you do!' She forced a bright smile to her lips. 'And you're right, Buttons will keep me company, won't you, sweetheart?'

Buttons reacted enthusiastically to her attention with some more manic licking.

'When do you have to leave?' she asked, keeping her eyes down.

'Tonight.'

'*Tonight*!' she gasped, her eyes snapping up.

'Yes. My flight leaves in a little over an hour. If I go immediately, there's still a chance I can get the rest of the stock flown over and into the stores before Christmas.'

'Are...are you packed?'

'Yes. I called Mrs Dawson from the office this afternoon.'

'She didn't say anything.'

'I asked her not to.'

'And when will you be back?'

'No later than next Thursday.'

'That long...'

'I should be finished in Tokyo within a few days but I'm going to drop off at Hong Kong on the way back.'

Juliana's stomach tightened. What had been the woman's name in Hong Kong? Jasmine, wasn't it? Jasmine... God, but that was a depressingly sensual and feminine name. No doubt Jasmine had everything else to match as well.

'So, what's the attraction in Hong Kong?' she asked a touch sharply.

'I have some business to do there as well.' He bent down to kiss her lightly on the cheek. 'I'll be as quick as I can.'

Juliana bit her tongue to hold her silence. She had no evidence that Blake was dropping off in Hong Kong to see some woman. He hadn't taken the address book last time he went overseas. Why should he this time?

Because you haven't been living as husband and wife for quite some time, came a darkly cynical voice. Not since a week before the *last* time he went overseas. Maybe he *needs* to see this woman.

'Blake!'

He was striding from the room when his name burst from her lips. Checking, he turned to frown at her obviously emotional outburst. 'Yes?' he asked. Almost warily, she thought. Or was it wearily?

She had wanted to tell him how much she would miss him, but suddenly the words would not come. 'Th-thank you for the puppy.'

His smile was definitely wry. 'My pleasure. *Au revoir*. Look after yourself, and don't go walking along deserted piers in the middle of the night.'

Within moments of his leaving, the terrible temptation to race into his room and see if that little blue book was still there gripped her in its tenacious hold and refused to let go. Juliana didn't know which would be worse—not looking and so keeping her optimistic hopes alive, or risking seeing that empty spot in the drawer.

In the end she could not stand the not knowing.

Clutching the puppy in her arms, she made her way shakily into Blake's room and opened the drawer. All the breath rushed from her body. It was there! Dear heaven, it was there!

She sank down on to the bed and buried her face into the pup's furry side, her whole body trembling with emotion. But gradually the strange feeling that

something wasn't quite right started wiping the
relief from her heart, replacing it with an increas-
ing unease. Lifting puzzled eyes, she stared once
again into that drawer.

And then it struck her. The book wasn't where
it had been before, peeping out from under the
novel. The novel was still there but the address book
was sitting on top of it in full view. Someone had
recently taken it out then put it back in a different
spot.

Why?

There were a host of innocent explanations, but
somehow Juliana wasn't comforted by any of them.
Finally, she put the pup on the bed, picked the
notebook up and started flicking through it again,
not knowing what that would prove, but doing it
anyway.

She saw the torn-out page straight away, and
knew, before a closer inspection confirmed it, that
it was the page which had included Jasmine from
Hong Kong. Pale but oddly composed now that she
knew the awful truth, she replaced the book, picked
up Buttons and returned to her room.

She sat on her bed, staring dry-eyed into space.

Five days, she had to think about all this. Five
days in which to make up her mind whether she
could live with, and continue to love, a man who
was unfaithful. Five days to find a way to survive
this utter, utter hell.

CHAPTER TWELVE

JULIANA lay back on the deckchair by the pool, doing her best to keep calm. Blake would not be home for a few hours yet. If she started becoming agitated now, she would be a mess by the time he arrived.

But it was hard to stay calm on the day one was going to ask for a divorce.

She had decided not to tackle Blake about Jasmine, or any of the other women in that book. Really, they were only a symptom of the true disease that was destroying their marriage, which was that Blake no longer trusted or respected her. She could have coped without his love. She could not cope with his lack of respect.

Buttons' sudden barking had her twisting round to see what was upsetting the little devil. Already that week he had chewed up two shoes, one fluffy slipper, the leg of a chair and anything else anyone left lying around. Susanne had forbidden him to come inside till he'd learnt to behave himself.

Juliana squinted over to where the barking was coming from. But the sun shining in her eyes made it difficult for her to see into the shadows of the wide patio. She could just make out someone sliding the glass doors back and scooping up the frantic animal, someone tall and...

The light glinting on his blond hair as he broke
out of the shadow sent a panicky rush of air into
Juliana's lungs.

'Blake!' She scrambled to her feet, hastily
drawing a see-through floral wrap over her brief
red bikini. 'What are you doing home this early?'

He came forward, idly stroking the puppy while
he frowned at her fluster. 'I caught an earlier flight.
Is there a problem with that? Are you going out?'
His narrowed gaze flicked over her scantily clad
form. 'You don't look as if you're going out.'

'No, I'm not going out, but I...I...' She was
floundering, for how could she say that she wanted
to be more formally dressed to face him with her
news?

'You what, Juliana? Have I come home at an
inopportune time? Is that it?'

His sarcasm was the last straw. Her eyes carried
total exasperation as they raked over him. She
shook her head in a type of weary frustration. 'Yes,
Blake,' she agreed grimly. 'You came home at an
inopportune time. I had a plan, you see, a time-
table in my mind. I was going to be so calm and
reasonable about everything. Mature and, yes...as
kind as I could be. Because I thought the way you
were was probably not your fault. But I can see
now that I would have been wasting my time. So
I'll just say it out straight. I want a divorce, Blake.
I can't take it any more.'

He said nothing for several seconds, his face
stiffly unreadable, his hand frozen mid-air above
the dog's head. Finally, he lowered the pup gently

on to the cement then straightened to glare at her. You can't take *what* any more?'

Juliana sighed. 'Not here, Blake. Not here...' And she turned to walk back towards the house.

His hand shot out to grab her arm, twisting her back to face him. 'Who is it?' he demanded to know. 'Tell me!'

She shook her head again in utter defeat. 'Please, Blake, I don't want a scene. I just want a divorce. You promised me we would call it quits after the first year if our marriage didn't work out. Well, the year's almost up and I'm not happy with you. That's the kindest way I can put it.'

His eyes widened with a look of dawning horror, his hand dropping from her arm. 'My God, you've fallen in love, haven't you?'

Her lips parted in surprise before she realised he meant fallen in love with someone else. But by the time she recovered her composure, the damage had been done. A guilty blush had already joined her goldfish gasp.

'It's not bloody Stewart, is it?' he ground out. 'Or Hawthorne again? For pity's sake, don't tell me it's Hawthorne!'

Juliana's eyes mirrored her deep sadness. 'It's no one, Blake. You've got it all wrong, as usual.'

'No, I haven't,' he pronounced with ironic insight. 'I've got it right, at last. You had an affair with someone while I was away those three weeks, and now you've fallen in love with him.'

Juliana stared up at him in total disbelief. 'Do you honestly think I would have been making love

with you the way I have been if I was in love with
someone else?'

'You *haven't* been making love to me lately! As
for those other times . . . you wouldn't be the first
woman to hide her guilt behind a burst of
passionate lovemaking. You probably hadn't fallen
in love with the bastard back then. It was probably
only another grotty little affair. For God's sake
why don't you admit it? You've already asked me
for the divorce. The least I deserve is the blood
truth!'

'All right, Blake. You want the truth? You can
have it. Yes, I have fallen in love with someone.
And yes, he is a bastard! You're so right about that
But you're wrong about the timing. I already knew
before our sex-life improved that I loved him. There
was no doubt in my mind at all. It was a certainty
And the reason it was a certainty was because my
secret love was none other than my own husband.
You, Blake! I'd fallen in love with *you*!'

All the blood had begun to drain from his face
during her speech, only to have colour jerk back
at the end.

'Me!' he exclaimed, clearly stunned.

'Yes, you.' Her laughter was only just this side
of hysterical. 'Funny, isn't it? Most men would
adore to have their wives love them as I realised
loved you, have *always* loved you.'

'You've . . . *always* loved me?' he rasped.

She shrugged with the sort of indifference de
spair brought. 'I didn't realise it till I thought you
might have died in a plane crash. It's amazing how
almost losing a person makes you aware of what

their value is to you. I...I...' She swallowed and tried to gather what inner resources she had left, looking up at two very shocked blue eyes with a growing bitterness. 'Yes, Blake, I've always loved you. Maybe from the very first moment we met.' Now her laughter was mocking. 'Blake Preston...my hero...my prince. Only my prince doesn't *want* my love. He never has. Love and he parted company a long time ago.'

'Juliana...darling...'

'Oh, don't "darling" me, you unfeeling, unfaithful rat!' she exploded, anger a much safer emotion than maudlin sentiment.

'Unfaithful!'

If she'd thought he was startled before, he was totally flabbergasted now. 'Since when have I ever been unfaithful?' he demanded, black clouds quickly gathering behind those momentarily wide eyes.

'Since you went to see your precious Jasmine in Hong Kong for starters!' she countered, and knew immediately by his face that she had hit the mark.

'Did you think I didn't know about your book of names?' she scoffed. 'Well, I did! Barbara was only too happy to tell me about them. She even told me where to find them. And I looked! Oh, yes, I looked more than once. It's amazing what a woman in love will do when she's desperate. And you almost got away with it this last time. If I hadn't noticed the rotten thing had been moved, if I hadn't picked it up and saw the page missing, I wouldn't have...have...'

Her voice trailed away when she found herself staring down at a small velvet box resting in Blake's outstretched hand. He also had the most peculiar look on his face, as though he was trying not to cry.

'Jasmine and I were once lovers,' he said shakily. 'A million years ago. All those women were my lovers . . . a million years ago. That book hasn't left my drawer for so long that I'd almost forgotten it was there till I had cause to look up a number again, the number of a certain woman who is married now but who is also a top jeweller. I needed Jasmine's number, Juliana, because I wanted to buy you this.'

And he flicked open the box to reveal an incredibly delicate but beautiful diamond ring. 'I never bought you an engagement-ring the first time round. I was going to court you properly this time, *make* you fall in love with me, because . . . you see . . . I had discovered how much I loved *you* the night you ran away. When I saw you lying unconscious in that hospital bed I knew that if you died, if I ever lost you, I would simply stop wanting to live . . .'

He dragged in a deep breath, letting it out with a shudder. But then his mouth curved back into a wry smile. 'Of course I had trouble admitting any of these radical feelings. How could I possibly have done the one thing I'd vowed never to do? Especially with my beautifully cool, independently ambitious wife, who didn't love me back, and who I mistakenly thought was having an affair, or affairs! I fought my feelings all that next week but, once I accepted that they wouldn't go away, that they were *real*, I decided to do something about them. Since you were still with me, I rationalised that this other man—or men—meant nothing to you. It was only sex. Yet *our* sex was better than ever! So I decided then and there that I would make you fall in love with me if it was the last thing I did. And now...now you tell me you loved me all along!'

Tears flooded Juliana's eyes. 'Oh, Blake...is it true? You really love me?'

'Do I really love her...?' He shook his head and for a split-second she saw a flash of pain that told her he'd been through as much hell as she had. Which he must have, she conceded, thinking all that time that she was being unfaithful to him, grappling with his jealousy, but still deciding that if he could win her back he would try to forget her infidelities and go forward.

He took the ring from its bed, tossed the box away then picked up her left hand. Both their hands were trembling. He slipped the diamond on her ring finger till it rested against the plain gold band.

'With this ring,' he said, 'I thee wed. With my body, I thee worship...'

And, sweeping her hard against him, he kissed her as though he would never let her go.

And he never did.

HARLEQUIN  PRESENTS®

It's getting hotter!

Look out for our sizzling selection of stories...

They're

Coming next month:

Dark Fire by Robyn Donald

Harlequin Presents #1735

From the moment they met, Flint Jansen had shattered Aura's world. She found him overwhelmingly attractive, powerfully charismatic...but she was already engaged to his friend Paul! She now faced a battle with her conscience, and with Flint: he demanded that she cancel the wedding and succumb to his dark seduction. In the heat of a tropical night, would Aura's resistance melt?

Available in April wherever Harlequin books are sold.

THTH-1

HARLEQUIN®

PRESENTS
RELUCTANT BRIDEGROOMS

Two beautiful brides, two unforgettable romances...
two men running for their lives....

My Lady Love, by Paula Marshall, introduces
Charles, Viscount Halstead, who lost his memory
and found himself employed as a stableboy by the
untouchable Nell Tallboys, Countess Malplaquet.
But Nell didn't consider Charles untouchable—
not at all!

Darling Amazon, by Sylvia Andrew, is the story of
a spurious engagement between Julia Marchant
and Hugo, marquess of Rostherne—an engagement
that gets out of hand and just may lead Hugo to
the altar after all!

Enjoy two madcap Regency weddings this May,
wherever Harlequin books are sold.

REG5

HARLEQUIN®

Don't miss these Harlequin favorites by some of our most
distinguished authors!
And now, you can receive a discount by ordering two or more titles

HT#25577	WILD LIKE THE WIND by Janice Kaiser	$2.99	☐
HT#25589	THE RETURN OF CAINE O'HALLORAN by JoAnn Ross	$2.99	☐
HP#11626	THE SEDUCTION STAKES by Lindsay Armstrong	$2.99	☐
HP#11647	GIVE A MAN A BAD NAME by Roberta Leigh	$2.99	☐
HR#03293	THE MAN WHO CAME FOR CHRISTMAS by Bethany Campbell	$2.89	☐
HR#03308	RELATIVE VALUES by Jessica Steele	$2.89	☐
SR#70589	CANDY KISSES by Muriel Jensen	$3.50	☐
SR#70598	WEDDING INVITATION by Marisa Carroll	$3.50 U.S. $3.99 CAN.	☐
HI#22230	CACHE POOR by Margaret St. George	$2.99	☐
HAR#16515	NO ROOM AT THE INN by Linda Randall Wisdom	$3.50	☐
HAR#16520	THE ADVENTURESS by M.J. Rodgers	$3.50	☐
HS#28795	PIECES OF SKY by Marianne Willman	$3.99	☐
HS#28824	A WARRIOR'S WAY by Margaret Moore	$3.99 U.S. $4.50 CAN.	☐

(limited quantities available on certain titles)

	AMOUNT	$
DEDUCT:	**10% DISCOUNT FOR 2+ BOOKS**	$
ADD:	**POSTAGE & HANDLING**	$
	($1.00 for one book, 50¢ for each additional)	
	APPLICABLE TAXES*	$_____
	TOTAL PAYABLE	$_____
	(check or money order—please do not send cash)	

To order, complete this form and send it, along with a check or money order for the
total above, payable to Harlequin Books, to: **In the U.S.:** 3010 Walden Avenue,
P.O. Box 9047, Buffalo, NY 14269-9047; **In Canada:** P.O. Box 613, Fort Erie, Ontario,
L2A 5X3.

Name: _____

Address: _____ City: _____

State/Prov.: _____ Zip/Postal Code: _____

*New York residents remit applicable sales taxes.
 Canadian residents remit applicable GST and provincial taxes.

HBACK-JM

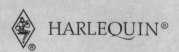
HARLEQUIN®

**AVAILABLE THIS
MONTH:**

ISBN 0-373-11728-0

$3.25 U.S.
$3.75 CAN.
March

HARLEQUIN PRESENTS®

MIRANDA LEE

Marriage i

Secrets

Everyone Has Something To Hide